S. 1

INTO THE

FOREST

 New Generation **Publishing**

This book is dedicated to my mum,
who always believed in me.

"There's no such word as can't."

Contents

"The forest is the dominant plant community and once it has occupied a locality it never leaves it."

Anon

"Suddenly I stop. But I know it's too late,
Lost in the forest, all alone.
The girl was never there, it's always the same.
I'm running towards nothing, again and again and again..."

The Cure, 'A Forest'

Prologue

The way she ran was unfocussed yet precise. She did not need her eyes and the darkness gave her shelter. No-one saw her and she saw nothing. But somehow she knew what she was doing, why she was running. To her sunken mind her destination was unclear, out of reach; to her feet it was obvious. When she stopped it was like hitting the brakes at the last possible moment and she almost fell, almost panicked. But instead she remembered everything.

Then she panicked. Then she fell.

1

Richard

Richard was happy. After all this time of wishing and dreaming it had finally happened. He was home at last. Out of the hectic noise and frustrations of the city and back in the land of trees and grass and birds and butterflies. He found himself smiling constantly, whistling, humming, sighing in sweet contentment at every glance through every window. The house was still chaotic of course, with boxes still to unpack and furniture parked hurriedly in ridiculous places; but he didn't care about that. All he cared about was being here.

He stood in the living room staring out into the garden and to the darkness of the forest beyond. The daylight had just begun to fade and the colours of the sky played in patterns across the landscape. The forest was unchanged and exquisite, a living echo of his boyhood memories. He had lived this moment so many times in his mind that it seemed entirely profound and set apart from reality. For a few exalted minutes he was truly incapable of moving, but then his eyes misted over and he closed them quickly, turning back to face the room and grinning at his good fortune. Before him, all was madness and confusion, but one quick glance over his shoulder and the world was a vision from his sweetest dreams. The temptation to return to that vision was almost irresistible but he knew if he did not resist he would be standing at the window all night! And besides, now he had the rest of his life to stare at his beautiful new world.

Still, Richard had no desire to begin the relentless

task of unpacking just yet. He could not conceive of spoiling his new-found joy with such tedious activities. What he really wanted to do was to go for a run: to feel the whisper of leaves at his side as his heart pumped and his lungs revelled in the lack of traffic fumes. No sirens or honking of horns, no shrieking gangs of youths emanating aggression, no drunks and junkies slowly shrivelling on benches, no pathetic heart-wrenching maniac yelling at thin air in some unfathomable language. The City was alive, yes, each second it pulsed with unstoppable energy, it was all that was real; but here, here at the edge of the forest was a land of fantasy. Here he had spent his carefree childhood. Here was where the sun always shone in the summer holidays, where the snow was always white for the sledging. Richard had decided a long time ago that this was where he truly belonged. City live was the buzzing of bees but here was the honey in the hive. He was happy, finally at peace, and as he meandered through the boxes towards the telephone he thought contentedly for the first time in his life that things really could not get any better.

He was right.

**

Katrina was out, again. Or of course there was always the possibility that she simply wasn't answering. After all, this was the fourth message he had left in as many days and still he had not heard back from her. He had been to the house on his way home from school but she had not answered the door and all seemed quiet inside. However, Richard was not really worried. Katrina was prone to disappearing from time to time and he also knew she could live for days without leaving the house and without speaking to a soul. Most of her friends were unaware of this as she preferred to let people think she was away on some exciting trip or simply too busy with her latest 'project' to take any calls. But Richard knew this was rarely the case and for the most part it didn't bother him that his girlfriend needed to shut the world out occasionally.

This time he was slightly puzzled though, and more than a little annoyed. Katrina had known full well when he was moving in and had promised to come round over the weekend for a night of celebration. And he had really wanted that first night to be special. It had still been special to him, but he had hoped that his moving here would be special for her too. She had seemed so happy for him and he remembered her assurance that they would spend so much more time together - so he had expected that she would be there waiting for him on Saturday morning, that she would help when the removal van arrived and share in his excitement as he revisited all his old haunts.

He sighed again and stared at the phone. "Ring for God's sake!" He forced himself to move away and tried to forget that it had been over a week since he had last seen her. She was bound to be all right. If he dared to admit it she was probably with some other man and he knew he should not be hurt by this. Katrina was fiercely independent and although they had been together for over two years she consistently and steadfastly refused to make any kind of commitment to their relationship. The idea was that they would always be there for each other but at the same time they were both free to see other people. Katrina was perfectly satisfied with this arrangement and could not understand why Richard was not. She had reassured him time and again that she would not be jealous if he took out, or even slept with, other girls and insisted that as long as they loved each other then 'meaningless sex' (as she put it) was completely irrelevant. Clearly, Richard could see the logic behind this theory but felt that in practise it did have certain flaws. Firstly, he was not at all sure that he understood the concept of 'meaningless sex'. Maybe he was a little old-fashioned but he had always believed that lovemaking was, well, making love - an act to be cherished between two people who truly cared for one another. He was aware that the majority of his male friends would disagree with him but the confusion arose in that most of his female friends, on the other hand, believed exactly as he did.

Katrina had laughed when he had tried to explain this, telling him that sex and love were not synonymous and that the two had been 'over-associated in the morals of society', whatever that meant. She had also refused to accept that he had never had a one-night-stand and said he must be very insecure if he needed her to be sexually faithful to him all the time! And that was the biggest problem - he knew that she wasn't. So although he honestly believed her when she assured him that he was the only man she really loved, he could not bear to think of her in the arms of another man – the thought made his fists clench of their own accord and his chest tightened with them until he could barely breathe. God she really drove him insane sometimes. Katrina Rose – the most impossible woman on earth! But he knew he would always love her. She had a magical quality that was hard to define yet impossible to overlook. That she was beautiful no-one would dispute, but there was something else as well. He had seen people totally unnerved by her presence, stammering when they were usually so eloquent, clumsy when normally so precise. Some of his friends would refer to her as "spooky chick" when they thought he couldn't hear. He had heard, of course, but it didn't bother him in the slightest, he knew where they were coming from. She *was* a bit spooky, but for him it only added to her charm. Besides, she was also undeniably intelligent, sensitive and yet spectacularly down to earth. Her unique brand of humour was born through a love of sarcasm capable of reducing him to immature fits of giggles and her mischievous mind was always ready to use this at the most inappropriate moments. He smiled now, thinking of the first time she had met his parents and how she had deliberately chosen to embarrass him with tales that were never meant for a mother's ears. But of course they had both simply adored her. When she needed to she could turn on that irresistible charm and get away with the most outrageous comments. He had even noticed her using it on him sometimes, and even though he knew exactly what she was doing he also knew he could do nothing but succumb to it.

Now, as he willed the phone to ring, he wondered what she would say to him this time, how she would hear his frustration and speak softly the exact words to soothe his temper. He could not be angry with her. He never had been, not really; she was too ... innocent, lost somehow, despite all evidence to the contrary.

Richard shook his head and went quickly into the kitchen. The phone would not ring while he stood and waited for it to ring. And it was obviously affecting his brain - Katrina innocent?! Surely he hadn't meant that. He ran the tap and splashed cold water on his face. He was the one who was lost if he could think of her as innocent for God's sake. He rinsed his mouth and made a conscious decision to forget about his so-called 'girlfriend'. She would call when she wanted to and that was that.

He looked up as he grabbed a tea towel to dry himself and stared out for the hundredth time across the garden and into the forest. He had kept himself busy with lesson-plans over the last couple of evenings but tonight he did not want to work. And if Katrina wasn't going to call him then he would do the other thing he had been most longing for since he arrived. He would go for a run in the forest.

2

The Forest

Blackhart Forest existed on any map as a small cluster of trees separating the towns of Blackleigh and Hartsbridge. It wasn't very big, as forests go, but it was still a forest and seemed endless in all directions. And it was perpetually dark. The sheer density of trees meant that even in the winter when the leaves were underfoot, the canopy let through only scatterings of light. Yet the shrubs and grasses flourished too, making the undergrowth as thick and impenetrable in places as the branches above them.

The forest was old and, for the most part, deciduous. Giant Oaks loomed majestically over their smaller companions of Hornbeam and Beech. Hawthorn and Elderberry sheltered in their midst and colours of violet and foxglove surprised the greenery as far as the eye could see. For Richard, it was the perfect time of year. Springtime was underway and the carpet of bluebells which grew only on the margins seemed a sight sent to welcome him as he stepped through the gate at the bottom of the garden.

He paused for a moment in a spell of nostalgia and then began to run. Slowly at first, his feet unaccustomed to the soft earth beneath them, but then faster and faster in a fury of joy. His mind had no sense of where he ran, but as he moved he became a boy again and he knew well the paths that he travelled.

He ran deeper into the forest, surrounded by noise and compelled by the quickening of his heartbeat. Its rhythm was hypnotic and as it pounded inside his head he realised he was running faster than he had done for years. He had to slow down, though he had no desire to do so, and as he forced his legs to obey he looked around him for the first time.

He had come to a small clearing where the forest tracks ended. He was not lost, but he caught his breath to realise that he had come so far. He was deep inside the Blackhart now and it was time to turn back. As a child he had learnt the lesson well and even the bravest boy warriors had not dared to pass beyond this point. As an adult, he knew that the stories of wolves and bears were impossible myths but he knew only too well why they had been created. From here the forest really came into its own and there were no more pathways to follow. To be lost in such territory would be just like a scene from one of those horror movies he had been so obsessed with as a teenager - stumbling forever in circles while the night closed in and the strange sounds of darkness surrounded him.

But Richard knew he need not bother with such morbid imaginings. He had no wish to discover how close to the truth they really were and he made up his mind to enjoy the run home at a steadier pace. Twilight was almost upon him and the forest seemed poised for the transformation. When they were kids his sister had called it 'Fairyland Time', and when the light faded such a title was apt in the extreme.

As he turned to retrace his steps he was startled from his reveries by the sharp snap of a twig behind him. He whirled round in surprise and saw the figure of a young girl standing in the shadow of a tall elm just beyond the clearing. She was still, silent, and though he could not see her face he had the distinct impression that she was staring straight at him.

"Hello?" Richard was more puzzled than nervous after the initial fright, but she did not answer him.

"Are you OK? Are you lost?" he ventured,

concerned now but still unnerved by her rigid stance. She appeared to him like a petrified animal, 'tharn' like a rabbit bathed in headlights or a deer at the crack of gunshot. He took a tentative step towards her and at once the spell broke. She stepped backwards and instantly disappeared behind the tree.

"Hey!" He yelled after her, "don't ..."

But she reappeared, just as suddenly, only now it was Richard's turn to stand frozen and the words dried up in his mouth. His spine was a tempest of spiders and somehow through the enveloping fear he heard a low moan escape from his lips as he felt himself grow hard beyond all control. He had no idea what was happening to him but he could not take his eyes from the vision before him.

Later, when he tried to remember the moment he could find no way to justify this intensity of dread and erotica. Yet he could not deny it. And for those few minutes, seconds even, he had no more mastery over his body than if he had been paralysed or encased in plaster. He was powerless and he sensed the power was all hers. And yet she did nothing. It was just a pose; a pose he had seen countless times on the city streets, on television screens, movie screens, the stereotype of whores everywhere. But she wasn't on any screen or under neon flashing lights, she was in the forest, and she was just a girl.

She remained in the shadows, the hour of the fairies now entirely upon them, but the shape of her body was perfectly and deliberately displayed. She had reappeared at the other side, in profile, leaning with her back against the rough bark of that same immense elm, one leg, the one closest to him, bent at the knee and the arm raised high above her head curling slightly round the trunk as if caressing its coarse texture. The breeze also knew its part in this timeless pose, gently floating her long hair away from her face and then back again, as though it too longed to touch and embrace but dare not lest the vision was dispelled.

Or perhaps the elements were actually under her command, for Richard felt no such breeze upon him. The air around him was as silent as he was, and he realised that the two of them were utterly alone. No creatures rustled in the undergrowth, no birds, no insects; the world had retreated as if it could not exist in a place so completely outside its comprehension. And although a part of him ached to follow such a retreat, still he could not move, and even if he could he knew he would not be able to leave her here. To turn and walk away was unthinkable. So he waited.

**

The girl had relaxed into her pose with no more thought than a professional hooker. She had no idea what she was going to do next but she had known, though she didn't know how, that to stand like this would hold him spellbound until she reached a decision. And of course it had worked. The problem now was that she couldn't make up her mind what to do with him. He obviously hadn't recognised her but then she had barely recognised him, even though she had known he was coming at his first step through the bluebells.

She remembered his name too: Richard Dean Haley, yet she could not remember her own. She did recall having a name at one time, but when she tried to think of it all she heard in her mind was that lilting, empty voice: "You're so pretty, so pretty, such a pretty girl." Over and over it had taunted her until she beat at her head with her fists that the pain would cancel it out. So she never thought about her name anymore. Hadn't for a long long time. It didn't matter now anyway, she

20

didn't need a name, she had the forest. And the Blackhart was her friend, her refuge. She loved it, and it loved her. She knew. No-one else had ever loved her like that. At least, she didn't think so. There was so much she couldn't remember. But that was all right. Everything was all right in the forest. At least it had been until the Blackhart had whispered one night that Richard Dean Haley was back.

She looked at him now, studied his face. It was no surprise that she had hardly known him, that he had shocked her so much when they had finally come face to face. She knew it had been a long time. Years, she thought, lots of years, though she could not count them. But she had not expected such a change in him. He was taller, broader than she remembered. He looked strong and fit, yet his skin was too white. She knew he had been to another place, but now she guessed it must have been somewhere far from here where the sun didn't shine enough and the people stayed inside all the time. His hair was another testament to this. When she had known him it was always slightly too long, always ruffled and always sun-bleached in natural streaks at the front. Now it was very dark all over, and someone had cut it too short so it was strange to see his ears for the first time. It made his face seem strange as well. The eyes were still blue but they seemed paler somehow, as though they had missed the sun as much as his skin, and he had deep lines on his forehead when he frowned. He was frowning now, as though in pain of some kind.

Suddenly, the girl found herself copying his frown. She hadn't hurt him had she? No, she would surely remember that. She remembered seeing that look on his face before, but only once, and she would not think about that. She would think instead about his smile. He had always smiled so much, been so happy. It was a nice smile, never false, and it was one of those quirky smiles, slightly off centre, as though one side of his face refused to cooperate in it. That's how she knew it wasn't really him that night, that night she would not think of.

She had to think of now, she knew that, but it was so hard to concentrate. She had tried to make plans but she had wanted so much to see him, as though she would know then, instantly, what she wanted to do. But instead she had just been frightened. Frightened like a child with the night-light turned off. Not of Richard. No, of course she could not be afraid of Richard. But maybe of the change in him, or of the fear he felt which she had sensed before he had even acknowledged it himself. No, it was something within herself that frightened her. Like now, the way the breeze blew against her face when she knew that there shouldn't be a breeze, wasn't a breeze. But maybe that was just the forest. She knew it liked to play games sometimes, just as she did.

There, that was it. The forest wanted to play a game. It was thinking of her as it always did. And so they would play a game. Games were always fun in the forest; all the children liked to play in the forest. But what should they play tonight? What would be the most fun? Richard always liked to play chase, she remembered, but she preferred hide and seek - there were so many wonderful places to hide. She really couldn't decide and she just hated having to think so much, it was such a long time since she'd had to do so much thinking. But that was OK, they could play them both.

The girl smiled and broke the pose. The spell was ended and as she darted off through the trees beyond the clearing she glanced only once over her shoulder to make sure that Richard was following.

**

Of course he was following. What other choice did he have? Was he really going to just ignore her and head off home with his mind full of pictures and questions? He was entranced. He was enthralled. He was excited, amazed, aroused, appalled, totally perplexed and, of course, more than a little terrified. But that wasn't true was it? He wasn't really afraid of some mysterious girl just because she . . . had done what exactly? She had done nothing. Well, apart from posing like some cheap street girl - and then the stillness and the breeze that wasn't there and the fact that she hadn't actually looked cheap at all. In fact she had looked, well, enchanting, like a dream of heaven on a starry night. And he had waited so long, it seemed, to see if this vision had a voice to soothe the anguish he could not control.

Richard ran with his thoughts, not caring now that he was in forbidden territory, caring only that he could still see flashes of her hair, her hand, her naked feet flicking skittishly under her peculiarly pale green dress. She dodged gracefully through the trees like a deer in flight and somehow he could not keep up. For all his speed he soon realised that she would not let him catch her. And she led him in patterns through invisible tracks, veering left to appear on his right and disappearing completely only to rustle from the ferns dead ahead.

And what of those ferns? Were they really silver like the bark of the birch trees surrounding them? And were they really all birch trees? Surely that was an Oak they just passed with the shimmering trunk and there was a Hornbeam with leaves that glittered, and how could there be Bluebells like a river before him when Bluebells just can't grow so deep in a forest like this?

And while we're on the subject, why was that Foxglove bathed in sunlight when he had seen the sun go down? And that rabbit was surely watching him. And the birds lining the branches stopped their singing as he ran past yet he could hear them calling behind him. Did it really sound like they were talking about him? And now where was she? She had been right there across the stream and he never knew there was a stream here but it seemed real enough and now she was gone.

Richard stopped and caught his breath. The girl was nowhere in sight and neither was he. He looked around, searching every distance but he already knew it was hopeless. This time she had lost him for good, and he was indeed utterly lost. He cursed out loud and almost screamed as he looked back at the stream only to find there was no stream after all.

Heart jumping wildly he stood for a moment and tried to think. He was truly scared now and could no longer deny it. And so confused he felt his head might burst from the turmoil going on inside it. But he knew this was not the time to try and figure everything out. For now he had to concentrate on getting out of here. And quickly, before the last of the fading light disappeared as surely as the girl had done - and the stream. He had been so sure there was . . . But no, he would not think about that now. He had to find a way back to that clearing, that was all. Surely they couldn't have come that far.

He turned around and tried to retrace his steps but found that nothing looked familiar. The circle of Silver Birches, the Bluebells, they all eluded him as he fought the panic and walked nervously through a landscape of perpetual sameness which chilled his soul until he felt he might collapse in despair. And he was so tired now that he almost *wanted* to collapse. Just to lie down for a minute and maybe he would wake up in bed . . . "Yeah and maybe you'd wake up dead" he told himself sternly, "keep walking".

He kept walking. The panic came and went like patches of ice as he stumbled through bushes he could barely see. He tripped constantly over tree roots, daring himself to fall and knowing if he did he would not stand up again. He stared always ahead of him, desperate for a pathway in the distance, and only when he realised he had walked without faltering for quite some time did he think to look down at the path he was already on. Amazed, he glanced around him and finally grinned in relief. This was the path from school he had used as a kid - the short-cut that all the kids had used and no doubt still did. If he hurried he'd be home in ten minutes.

With an improbable burst of energy and a silent thank you to a God he wasn't even sure existed Richard settled into a steady jog for the short journey home. He kept his eyes on the path and tried to think about Katrina, or his fantastic new house, or even work. But he couldn't. All he could think about was the girl, the stream, and the forest - which for the first time in his life he was glad to be leaving.

3

Katrina

Katrina sighed and lit another cigarette. He would be back soon and she wasn't worried anymore. For a while there she had thought maybe something was wrong but the feeling had lifted and she was sure he would not be long now. And she was quite content to wait here on the step outside the back door, staring at the long grass and all the weeds in his untended garden. She knew he would tame it all too quickly, with a short tidy lawn and neat rows of flowers around the edge - and probably a nice straight path of paving stones stretching right down to the quaint wooden gate at the bottom. He was always so organised like that. And though she loved his practical ways she knew she would always prefer the garden as it was now. It seemed more beautiful somehow, in its freedom.

But now the light was gone and the colours with it. The whole place looked different in black and white, not nearly so pretty, and the forest beyond looked menacing in the gloom. She hated the Blackhart anyway, and with good reason, but she did not care to think about those reasons anymore.

She looked at her watch and thought 'five minutes'. This was a precise message which she trusted implicitly, though she would not have been able to explain why. It was just a sense she had. All her life she had learned to rely on these instincts, and they had never lied to her. Richard always laughed and called it coincidence, her girlfriend Jenny said she was psychic. Katrina herself believed that everyone could do it if they wanted, only most people ignored it so much that they finally ceased to notice it altogether.

Tonight her instinct had told her that Richard needed her. That and the countless messages on her answering machine, of course! But until tonight Jenny had needed her more than he had. She had had yet another row with her rotten boyfriend and, as usual, Katrina had taken her in and tried to convince her that he was no good, that she should leave him for ever this time. She was still at her house even now, with strict instructions not to answer the phone or the door to the slimy bastard. But he would get to her anyway; all tears and apologies while she packed up her things and went back to him - until the next time.

Thank God Richard wasn't like that. But then she would never be with any man who treated her so badly. Richard was quite amazing actually, she had to admit. In fact, she was the one who treated him badly, no matter how much she loved him. And she did love him. She loved him more than anyone or anything in the world. The other men she slept with were nothing compared to him, yet she cared for them too in her own special way. It was a problem she could not find a solution to, and she was sorry for it. Yet she could not change, and whenever she thought about it she really did not see why she should change. Why should society's rules be 'right'? Why did people insist that if you truly loved someone you would never even *want* to have sex with anyone else? The idea was ridiculous to her. Did other people really feel like that? She didn't think so. She'd seen the way her friends were and the only reason they stayed faithful to their partners was a simple one - fear. As in: "He'd kill me if he found out", or "She goes mad if I so much as look at another woman". No, they all wanted to. They even fantasised about their object of lust while they made love to their respective boyfriends and girlfriends. And surely that was worse. Not only was it deceitful but it meant denying your true feelings. And yet there was an answer to that theory too. She knew all the arguments: "You should be prepared to make sacrifices for the one you love", "deny those feelings out of respect for your partner", etc etc. And maybe those answers were right. Maybe she was just making excuses for her own hedonistic behaviour.

She breathed in deeply as if to stifle the confusion. Richard was so wonderful to her. He put up with all her moods and her strange bouts of reclusion. And he did know about the other men, he'd even tried to understand on the few occasions when they'd talked about it. But mostly he just pretended it wasn't happening. That way he didn't have to deal with it. She wondered if that's what he was thinking about now, if that was why he'd gone off on one of his runs. She knew that was where he was. Even as she had rung the doorbell she had seen him deep in her mind somewhere, running through the forest like the devil himself was chasing after him. And in that hellish place she could almost believe it.

Katrina shivered slightly and recalled the sensation she had had earlier. It had only lasted a few minutes but for that short time she had been convinced that Richard was in trouble; that she would never see him again except in a coffin at some lousy funeral service before they burnt his body to a fine silvery powder. Morbid thoughts indeed for such a hard-core hedonist like herself. But the feeling had passed and she knew now that she would see him - she checked her watch - in two and a half minutes, give or take the odd second.

She smiled at the thought of his return. Red-faced and panting in his sweat-streaked T-shirt and running shorts, muscles hard and gleaming from their unexpected workout. And he would be so surprised to see her here, waiting to pounce when his eyes sparkled with that oh so charming half-smile he was all too aware of. And she knew she would pounce. She had missed that smile, that gorgeously toned body and those amazing arms that seemed to engulf every part of her being. And she would love to make love to him right here in the garden, deep in the grass and the dandelions, the cool air on her naked breasts, leaves tickling her neck. But that was just wishful thinking. He would want a shower and a coffee, and definitely an explanation as to why she hadn't returned his calls or been round to help him unpack. Well he could have all of that. And he would understand about Jen and he would probably even apologise for being angry and he would be so sweet and so kind that she would wonder again what she had done to deserve such a beautiful man. And then they would make love, and that too would be a taste of heaven - but she would still go over to Steve's tomorrow. Steve who was so unlike Richard that they could be from a different species. Steve who had handcuffs and chains, who told her what to do and when to do it, who fucked her like it was war until she screamed from a pleasure so painful she didn't know which it was anymore. She needed this roughness sometimes, just like she needed Peter with his games and her silky underwear. And maybe if she could do all that with Richard she wouldn't need them at all. But with Richard it was different. They rarely had sex, they just made love. And he would not do anything that might hurt her even if she asked him to. It just wasn't in his nature. He could be adventurous in his way, and he was an excellent lover, sensitive and tireless till she forced him over the edge. But always he was gentle.

She sighed again and stared out across the wilderness of lawn. He was almost home, her sweet and gentle Richard, and tonight he was the only lover she wanted.

**

She watched him arrive, a hazy silhouette fumbling with the latch, and then the slow march up through the garden, head down and deep in thought. Halfway to the door he looked up and noticed her, clearly for the first time. He was more than surprised. For a second she thought that was fear in his eyes, but that was crazy, and then came the smile she had been waiting for. He came to her quickly then, just as she hurried to greet him, and suddenly she was in his arms and he was kissing her, his cold lips covering her face and neck with an urgent desire unlike any he'd ever shown before. Still shocked she returned the passion, unable to stifle a small cry as he ripped at her shirt and tore away the buttons. His strength was brutal, unchecked, and Katrina all but fell to the ground as he tugged at her jeans and came down heavily upon her. There were no soft caresses, no murmurs of love as he held her there, and then he thrust into her, hard and sharp, and she heard their frenzied groans as if from afar.

She may have screamed at some point, she couldn't quite remember. Her brain seemed to have switched itself off and now she was having trouble wiring it up again. She concentrated on refocusing her eyes and turned to look at Richard - but he too was out of focus, lying still and unreachable in the flattened grass at her side, eyes closed yet frowning visibly with those little creases on his forehead. She moved the glance downwards and almost laughed aloud at what she saw. Her mind awoke with a click that felt somehow tangible as she stared at the red marks on her breasts and the bundle of denim still attached to one ankle. Had that really been Richard? Were those really Richard's teeth that had left her nipples with that bruised, tingling sensation? Katrina sat up and looked at him again in open wonderment. He looked unbelievably sexy to her, lying naked in the dark garden, one arm slung casually above his head, the other clenched tight into a fist around a clutch of long grass. And of course that delicious sex scent still surrounded him, hanging in the air as though it too was reluctant to admit that it was all over. But it was over. And no matter how much she would love an action replay it was definitely time to go inside now. The sky was black, clouds blocking the stars, and all at once she acknowledged the cold and noticed the goose bumps on her exposed skin. And Richard was too pale now, still frowning. Obviously she had been right to be worried earlier.

"Richard?"

It was the first time either of them had spoken and the sound of her voice seemed strange, too loud.

She bent slightly and stroked the side of his face. "Come on, it's getting cold."

His eyes opened (was that the same flash of fear?) and the frown vanished as he smiled up at her. And was that a sigh of relief as he sat up beside her? But he just laughed at the disarray of clothes as she had wanted to and then began to gather them all up.

"Yeah," he said finally, "I think we could both do with a shower."

4

The girl

The girl sat alone by the stream, her back warm against the solid trunk of her favourite tree. As always she was comforted by the life-force within it, the sap pulsing, rhythmic, like a slow strong heartbeat deep inside. She drew her feet up and leant further into it, as though she was trying to push herself into the very soul of the life behind her. She needed this reassurance now, for she was unsure about what she'd just done. She knew Richard was home safe, so that was all right. She had watched him all the way just to be sure, nudging him gently in the right direction. She was still mildly puzzled as to how she was able to do this, both the watching and the nudging; something at the back of her mind told her that she shouldn't really be able to do either. But she could, so there wasn't much point in thinking about the how part. She had found it was always best not to think about the things that she didn't understand, and then they didn't matter anymore.

The girl was tired but she would not let herself sleep just yet. That was why she had come to sit by the stream like this - it always made her want to pee, and as long as she needed to pee she knew she wouldn't sleep. And she must try and remember first, then she could sleep.

The problem was that she couldn't really remember very much at all. She remembered watching him stumble around before he saw the pathway, and then suddenly falling into a slow run when he realised he wasn't lost. She remembered seeing the gate, hazy and grey beyond the bluebells, and feeling like she wanted to go on, to go through the gate with him and see into the garden which she knew must lie beyond. But she hadn't been able to do that. She had tried her best but it had just ended, SNAP, and she was back here in the Blackhart. And that was OK. It was good, really, that she had to stay here, amidst all this wonderful life and love. And besides, where would she go if she could get out? She would only be lost and frightened, just like Richard had been earlier. She could still sense the pain of his fear, even now, but she couldn't think what he had been so frightened of.

She sighed and hugged her knees, resting her forehead on her thighs. Maybe he had just got lost and that's what had scared him so much. It's not as if he could have been scared of her. She was sure she hadn't done anything to him. She had looked at him, she knew that much, and then she remembered running and dancing and feeling happy. But that was all. And then she had let him go, watched him go. Had she meant to let him go home like that? She decided she must have meant it otherwise he would still be here. But if he was here he would still be scared, and that wouldn't be right, he wasn't supposed to be scared. So maybe that's why she had let him go home.

It was a good decision and the girl lifted her head, feeling proud of herself. Richard was all right, she had not hurt him and she had watched him get home safe and sound. And that meant he would come back again, the forest would tell her when he was here and she could see him again and he wouldn't be scared of her and everything would be OK. So now she could go and pee and finally go to sleep and even if she couldn't remember when she woke up she would know everything was all right or she wouldn't be waking up because she would still be awake.

5

The gift

"I thought you were going to stay in there all night."

Richard just smiled and shrugged at her.

"I made some coffee but yours is probably cold by now. It's on the side in the kitchen."

He mumbled a 'thanks' at her as he started down the stairs and again she wondered if he was all right. He had hardly spoken a word since they came inside and had insisted on showering alone; not unusual in itself but he had been strangely defensive about it, and he didn't usually stay in there for half an hour either. She watched him descend the stairs and noticed again how exhausted he looked. But she held her tongue for the moment - it was time to get those grass seeds out of her hair.

Katrina moved thoughtfully towards the bathroom, her eyes lingering on the hallway where Richard had just disappeared. She noticed her car keys on the window ledge and in the same moment as she asked herself why she had come around in the car she suddenly remembered exactly why and stopped dead in her tracks.

"Oh my God!" She ran down the stairs and grabbed the keys, shouting for Richard who rushed into the hall fearfully, relaxing only when he saw Katrina's face.

"You won't believe what I've gone and done." She was half upset, half amused. "I've left your present in the bloody car!"

"What present?" He went towards her as she opened the front door and looked back at him.

"All this time, poor thing, I can't believe I forgot."

She was already out of the door as Richard repeated

"poor *thing*?" In utter bafflement. He held the door open and watched as she pulled a cardboard box from the front seat. And then he heard it. The tiny plaintive mew of a kitten.

"Oh Kate," he stood there beaming at her as she struggled to close the door with the box in her arms. The kitten continued to mew and Richard finally went to help her, clutching the little box to his chest protectively. He was completely soppy over cats, always had been, but he had not wanted one in the city; it just didn't seem right to keep a cat cooped up indoors all the time and he certainly wouldn't have let it loose amongst the cars and the psychos. But here, here was the perfect place for a cat - especially with the Blackhart so close with all the trees to climb and wildlife to chase. He had a twinge of bizarre discomfort at the thought of the forest but it left him in a split second and he was all anticipation as he put the box gently on the floor, crooning softly "it's OK little one, OK kitty cat".

He looked up, slightly embarrassed as he noticed Katrina grinning down at him, eyebrows raised to mock him. But all she said was "I bought all the stuff to go with it as well, it's all in the car. Is he OK?"

Richard opened the box carefully and found himself staring wondrously down at the tiniest, blackest, most sorrowful looking kitten he had ever seen. It stared straight back up at him with startling blue eyes and mewed right at him, just once. And that was that: for the second time in his life, Richard Haley had fallen in love.

6

Bethany

Katrina sat on a stool in the kitchen and sipped at her coffee. The house was quiet and the sun was a streak of yellow through a gap in the curtains. Richard had left for work, of course, which is why the curtains weren't wide open - Katrina had yanked them closed, eyes squinting, as soon as he'd walked out of the door. She wasn't at her best in the mornings, in fact she wasn't usually awake in the mornings, but when she was the last thing she needed was a bloody bright light shining in her face. Unfortunately, Richard was the exact opposite. He was definitely a morning person, in inverted commas. He would wake up instantly at the first hint of daylight, and to Katrina's constant incomprehension, it made absolutely no difference how much, or how little, sleep he had had the night before.

Last night they had had very little sleep. After the excitement of Frankie, the newly named kitten (his idea - Frank Sinatra / Blue Eyes - even though she had told him that all kittens had blue eyes and they would soon change) Richard had finally been able to relax, and then they had spent hours just talking.

It had started with apologies. Katrina explaining about Jenny and sensing the tightly hidden relief when he learnt that she hadn't been with another man after all. But she should have called him, that was all he said in the end, and she had agreed, "Yes I know, I'm sorry, I guess I was just so wrapped up with Jen." But afterwards she had thought there was more to it than that. Had she, on some level, *wanted* him to think that she was with a lover? She had dismissed that idea last night, it seemed so cruel, but now, thinking again, she really could not be sure. Except to know that it wouldn't happen again.

She drank more coffee, it was cool enough now, and wondered again why Richard put up with her. 'Because he loves me' came the unbidden answer, and she knew it was true. The thought made her smile despite the early hour and she remembered laughing when Richard had made his unexpected apology. He had been quite uncharacteristically embarrassed: "I'm, um, sorry about, er, in the. . y'know . . earlier, in the garden. I was too rough, I guess, and um.." Her spluttering laugh had stopped him there. She had tried not to let it out in case he realised why it was so funny to her, but all she could think was 'rough, my God, if only you knew!' Of course she hadn't said anything like that, that really would be cruel, but she had told him to feel free to do it again, that she had hoped he would take her in the garden, that it was good, that it was sexy, that she loved him.

They had talked about love for a while, about each other, about friends, other couples, and then about Richard's new job in his old school (very strange), the house, plans for the garden (she had smiled at his idea for a path down to the gate), and finally about the forest. She hadn't been sure if he would tell her that night, she would have been prepared to wait, but it had been clear that something was weighing on his mind. So she had listened.

He had told it like a story, eloquent and detailed, which she supposed was a natural reaction - especially for someone who spent half of his time immersed in books. And for the most part he had told it entirely without emotion, as though it really was a story, and not something that had happened *to him* only a few hours earlier. He looked at her only when he had finished, and he faltered just twice. The first time was when he was describing what he had called 'the pose', which took three attempts whilst he tried to convey feelings which he himself barely understood, and the second was the bit about the stream. It was obvious to her that he had considered leaving both these incidents out of the telling, but at the same time these were the two things he needed to tell the most. He was shaking by the end, desperate to conceal it, and she had left him for a moment with the excuse of making them both another drink.

In truth she hadn't known what to say. She recalled making some flippant remark to lighten the mood, something along the lines of "no wonder you needed a good shag", but that was as much for her benefit as for his. The whole thing had really unnerved her, and of course it had made her think of Bethany - a subject she avoided as much as possible.

Bethany had been gone for nearly fourteen years now, but the pain hadn't gone at all. It was strange really, she had never liked her sister, she used to tell people she hated her, wished she'd never been born - and maybe that part was true. But actually it was completely impossible to hate Bethany. She was always such a happy girl, kind and loving to everyone, always wanting to please, wanting to be loved and loving life for those simple pleasures. Katrina was the only reason she ever cried because Katrina ignored her completely, told her she was stupid and annoying and "don't you ever come into my room again!" She had only spoken to her to yell and to call her names and to make her go away, but Bethany had never given up. She always ended up crying and confused but the next day she would try again, and the next day, and the next. It went on like that for years. Until that final day when everything went wrong.

Katrina had grown up a lot by then, they both had, and she thought she understood her feelings and could recognise that it was her father she was angry with and not her sister. So she had decided to talk to her at last, to tell her that it was OK, that they were sisters and that she did love her after all. But those words hadn't come out. She had found different words instead, closer to the surface, a lifetime of jealousy and resentment unleashed in a moment of exquisite release. Those words were gone too now. It was just the face she remembered, and the tears and the running; but Bethany didn't have the asthma and the pack a day habit to slow her down. She had run into the forest, to a place she called her refuge, her place of peace, and Katrina could not catch her.

So afterwards she had sat in her sister's bedroom and waited. She had thought it would be OK. When Bethany came home they would talk properly and this time she would say the right words, she would say "I'm sorry, I love you, you're my sister". She still dreamt about that sometimes, but a dream was all it could be. Bethany had run into the Blackhart for the last time, and Katrina had never seen her sister again.

The tears had come unbidden and unnoticed through the memories and Katrina brushed them away angrily. She hated to cry and was instantly glad she was alone. It had been a long time since she had thought so clearly of that terrible night and she wondered at such an unusual lack of self-control in allowing it. All that talk of the forest had been even more disturbing than she had realised, especially as Richard had seemed so convinced of the unlikely events which had transpired there. He had assured her that he hadn't really been frightened at any point but Katrina knew male bravado when she heard it and was well aware of the level of fear he had experienced. She had felt it herself while she had waited for him, and had seen it sharp in his eyes on his return, although even she hadn't wanted to admit it at the time.

But now it was Katrina's turn to be scared. She had listened with increasing amazement as Richard had described the 'barefooted girl', as he called her, realising that in every detail he was describing someone she knew far too well. But it could not be possible. The girl he had described was lost forever and though Katrina had always clung to the reassuring instinct which told her that the sister she had wronged was still alive, she had also always assumed that this was a false instinct born of guilt and anguish.

Now she did not know what to think. As far as she was aware Richard had no idea she even had a sister, never mind be able to describe her looks to perfection - and her playful personality for that matter. The whole mischievous chase through the woods was just the type of game Bethany would love, and she had always been so fast and agile that it was possible she could outmanoeuvre even an experienced runner like Richard, especially if he was as disorientated as he had portrayed.

But of course it was still impossible. Bethany would be twenty-eight now if she were still alive, not the small and slender fourteen year old she had been back then. And it was certainly the young Bethany who Richard had described with such uncanny accuracy, so unless it was her ghost ...

But Katrina could not bear to think of that. She was not really sure which way her beliefs lay on the subject of ghosts but she knew it was unbearable to believe that her sister was anywhere but one of two places: alive and well and living a new life somewhere, or dead and at peace, finally happy in the knowledge that her big sister did love her after all.

Katrina sat and sobbed bitterly. She could no longer hold back the pain and the tears as she allowed herself to grieve once again for the sister she had lost. She had not cried for Bethany for many years and the release was overwhelming. Finally it was Frankie who snapped her out of it. He had been sleeping in a tight black ball all morning but he woke with a tiny yawn and scampered out of his bed straight across to where Katrina was sitting. She heard a small mew and then screamed "Ouch!" as he used her leg like a tree trunk and clawed his way up to her lap.

"You little rat!" She yelled, sniffing, "That bloody hurt, you know?" Frankie just looked at her, head on one side, practising his cutest innocent kitten face. "And that won't work on me either, Ratboy, I have a version of that face myself so I know exactly what you're up to." The kitten, clearly not fazed by his new nickname, just rolled over, purring, and rubbed his face into her hand. Katrina smiled against her will and stroked his head. She dried her eyes on the sleeve of her dressing gown and suddenly decided she would not go to Steve's place today.

"Come on Ratboy, time to sort this house out. I want everything looking perfectly organised and boring by the time your dad gets home."

She picked up the kitten and placed him gently on the floor. There was a lot to tidy up from last night and plenty of boxes to unpack so Katrina set to work, intent on keeping herself so busy that she would have no time at all to sit and brood over the past or to ponder over Richard's adventure in the Blackhart. As she walked into the living room the brightness from outside attracted her gaze and she marched purposefully over to the window to shut out the unwelcome glow. She had intended simply to draw the curtains but on reaching them she found herself glaring harshly at the forest with such animosity that she could barely tear her eyes away. In that moment she felt a hatred for the Blackhart so intense that it terrified her, and she did not draw the curtains but yanked them across so aggressively that she was surprised she didn't rip them off the rails completely.

Katrina clenched her fists and closed her eyes. She breathed in deeply and forced herself to relax, letting out a long sigh as she let her eyelids open slowly to survey the room before her. It was in total chaos; glasses and mugs and clothes and boxes and a small black kitten happily shredding an envelope all over the settee. She smiled and switched the light on. It was going to be a busy day.

7

School

Richard's first day of teaching in his old school was going very well, all things considered. Despite his liveliness in the morning, he began to feel increasingly tired throughout the day and the strange events of the previous night were never far from his thoughts, making it ever harder to concentrate on the lesson plans he had so carefully arranged over the weekend. He did enjoy being back at work, however, and he found the children here quite different from the City kids he had taught before. They seemed so much more laid back and were easier to quiet at the start of class. In fact, many of them even seemed interested in what he was teaching, rather than texting their friends under the desk when they thought he wasn't watching.

He was used to young teenagers and the various tricks they pulled and all the backchat they suddenly felt adult enough to engage in, but for some reason the children here weren't giving him any trouble at all. He stayed alert and assumed the next class would provide the problems but each time he was wrong, until he finally realised there would be no troublemakers today at all. It was as though he was teaching a younger age-group altogether and he felt glad that these kids were hanging on just that bit longer to their carefree childhood.

Of course, he also assumed that he was just having a particularly easy day and that tomorrow or the next day the bright but insolent ones would have noted his weaknesses and begun to play on them.

But he decided that he would enjoy it whilst it

lasted. And he decided too that tomorrow he would make a concerted effort to stop staring so much at all the girls faces to see if he could find the barefooted wench he had lost in the forest; for he was convinced now that it was just a young teenager playing games with him to shake him up a little. His logical mind told him that there could be no other explanation, and the confusion with the stream and everything else was just an illusion created by his becoming lost and disorientated - which was so easy in a place like the Blackhart.

So Richard enjoyed his day and remembered only the excitement of the run and the thrill of being back in his beloved forest again. He laughed inwardly at himself for being so afraid of a mere girl and of being lost in a place which he had all but lived in as a child. Classes had finished and it did not matter that he hadn't seen the girl. She may not be in any of his classes anyway, or perhaps she would just look so different in a school uniform or with her hair tied back that he would never recognise her at all. And though he was sure he would not see her in the forest again either, as he gathered his books and notes to take home his excitement grew in anticipation of his evening run. He thought he would go into the forest again, there was a really good route he could take past a small clearing which he thought he could find quite easily.

8

The girl

Whilst Richard taught his classes and Katrina organised his house, the girl sat on the stump of an old dead Oak Tree and battled with her memory.

She knew that Richard was back and that she had played with him last night, but she felt there was something important about his return that she was supposed to recognise. There were only two names she remembered from her past: Richard Dean Haley and Katrina Rose. Katrina was to be protected at all costs, and Richard was to be ... to be what? She knew she had been waiting for his return for such a long time but she just couldn't remember why. She had always adored him but she felt sure she had loved many people and she just wished she could remember why he was so significant to her.

She stroked the young hare on her lap absentmindedly and healed his wounded leg. She had no idea how she could do this but had accepted it as a gift which she must use to keep the forest and it's inhabitants healthy and strong. The sick and wounded always found their way to her so she just sat with them and talked to them and loved them and then soon they went away, happy and well again. But they would always come back to her if she was lonely or sad. It was as if the whole forest was in tune with her feelings and wanted to help. She believed that this was true, that the forest loved her as much as she loved it, that it wanted to protect and cherish all who dwelt there, that as long as she remained within it's boundaries she would be safe and happy.

But she wasn't happy. In fact she wasn't sure if she had ever been happy at all. Yet how would she ever know, with her memory as dreadful as it was. Maybe she had once been blissfully happy all the time but she just couldn't remember it.

The girl sighed and looked down at the small creature sleeping peacefully under her spell. His leg was on the mend now and he would be fine to run again in a couple of days. Until then he would stay with her and she would care for him and keep him safe. She placed him gently in a bed of dry grass and ferns she had made earlier. He was quite well hidden in a tiny natural cave of entwined tree roots and she rubbed the scent from her hands all around to ensure no other animal would dare to enter. They all knew that any place marked by her smell was strictly out of bounds except by invitation and she knew her patient would be perfectly safe for the rest of the day. As for herself, she had decided that the only way to try and recapture her memory was to visit the strange enclosure in the sycamore tree which she had found some time ago. It was old and broken now, but when she had first come across it she had seemed to recognise the familiar structure and had become too upset to linger there. She had not been back since then, but somehow she had never forgotten where it was, nor had she forgotten the colourful bag which she had discovered hidden in a spidery corner. The bag had been full of things she had not understood, things which she had wanted to read but which had left her with a queasy stomach and watery eyes. She had known that it was very important, that it contained the key to another life, so she had re-hidden it carefully before making her swift retreat and she hoped that she would be able to find it once again. Maybe it belonged to one of the giggling girls she saw walking together through the forest path, always so happy on their way to the 'outside'. They went one way in the morning and then back again the same afternoon, all following the same path and all following each other like birds migrating back and forward each day.

She sometimes thought that she remembered where they were going but it was so hard to think of the 'outside'; her head would start to throb and if she concentrated too hard she would get sick and start to shake. She had thought the 'outside' must be truly horrible to cause such a reaction but obviously the others she saw were quite happy to go there, so now she had just given up trying to understand. Clearly her place was here and that was all that was important. Except now this nagging question about Richard Dean Haley. It was driving her mad, constantly flashing his face and his voice into her mind and spoiling her dreams at night. She had to remember or she would get no peace at all.

Satisfied that the hare was secure, the girl set off at a light run and began to move away from the centre of the Blackhart where she spent most of her time. It was a long way to where she must go and as she ran she felt a nervous flutter in her belly - was that fear she was feeling? She vaguely remembered feeling this before but as usual she did not know when or why. But she had to go on now. The forest compelled her to keep moving as if it too was desperate for her to remember and her feet knew the way without consulting her anxious mind and soon she was flying through the trees and bushes faster than she had ever run and her heart pounded and her eyes watered and still she ran and ran - and then suddenly she stopped.

Panting heavily she collapsed exhausted to the floor, laying unbeknown to her exactly as she had lay that very day fourteen years ago when she had awoken to the sound of footsteps and shouting. The girl finally took in her surroundings and sat up in awe as she realised that this was the first time she had come back to this spot since she had begun her life in the forest. She felt sick and dizzy and wanted desperately to run away again, to be anywhere but here. She noticed that there were tears streaming down her face and she was making strange choking sounds which she did not recognise. This was a bad place, it spoke to her only of terror and pain and confusion, and she knew she would have to gather all her strength to stay here and do what she had come to do.

As she cried the creatures of the forest came slowly forward to comfort her. The old fox she had healed as a cub and kept away from the evil huntsmen all these years, and the small roe deer she had nursed when he had come to her last spring with a nasty bite from an adder he had disturbed. They all came: rabbits, field mice, tiny shrews and of course all the different birds which flocked above her. Every branch was filled with singing and the fluttering of wings, each one trying to reassure and calm their healer. The animals had no more concept of what they were doing than the girl ever did, but they knew that the forest wanted them here with her, and so they came.

Gradually, the girl calmed her tears and allowed the forest to soothe her. She went very slowly and apprehensively to the tree-house where she had hidden her belongings all those years ago. She knew now that this had been her own private refuge in times of trouble, that the bag and its contents had actually belonged to herself in her previous life, and as she found it again she found her memories too. Some were welcome, others were so painful she screamed and quickly locked them away. But at last she knew everything once more and, as she felt Richard take his first steps into the Blackhart, she smiled, this time more sinister than playful, and the animals scattered as she darted to the clearing to wait for him. This time, thought Bethany, she would really have some fun.

9

The run

Richard had hurried home, his excitement growing out of all proportion, and bolted upstairs to change without even realising that his front door had not been locked or that Katrina was still in the house. He was focussed only on the expectation of seeing the girl in the forest and his heartbeat had already begun to quicken in anticipation.

The sight of Katrina laying sleepily on his bed, therefore, made him jump so much he had to sit down to catch his breath.

"What's going on?" She mumbled, still drowsy. Richard could not help grinning after his initial shock, she looked so tousled and slow.

"Just going for a run sweetie, didn't realise you were here. You almost gave me a heart attack!" He walked over to the wardrobe and began to undress. Katrina sat up and watched him, a worried expression on her face.

"I suppose you're going in the forest again?"

"Of course! I'm hardly going to run round the streets when the Blackhart is right there in all its glory." He turned to look at her, slightly puzzled by the tone of distress he had detected, and was shocked to see tears in her eyes and a strange look of dejection he had never seen her wear before.

"Jesus hon, what's wrong?" He rushed over to comfort her and she wrapped her arms around him tightly. His concern was genuine as he had known Katrina for many years and had never once seen her cry, but he also found himself slightly annoyed that the run he was so desperate for was being delayed.

"Come on sweetie, what's going on?" He asked gently, but she did not give him a direct answer. Instead she practised her most endearing expression and beseeched him to stay at home tonight.

"I mean, you can go for a run anytime but I thought I would cook dinner for you and we can get a DVD or something and I tidied the whole house today specially so why don't you just come downstairs and put your feet up and then everything will be OK, OK?"

Richard stared at her as though she had lost her mind completely. For a start Katrina never, ever cooked. She didn't even make toast or a sandwich or even boil the kettle for that matter. And tidy the house? That was so utterly unheard of that something must be very wrong. His first thought was that she was feeling guilty about something but she must have read it in his eyes for she suddenly burst out "I haven't done anything stupid I just don't want you going in that bastard forest that's all! I just have this dreadful feeling that something really bad's going to happen to you and after what happened yesterday I just don't think you should be going back there. I know it sounds mad but can you please just trust me on this? You know I'm always right with these feelings?"

Richard knew all too well about Katrina's 'instincts' and 'feelings'. He had seen them proved right on many occasions but for some reason he still continued to be sceptical because that was his way of dealing with anything he could not explain. And besides, this time he was convinced that she was simply overreacting. After all, last night he had been a tiny bit scared himself, before he came to understand that nothing bizarre had actually happened at all, that he had obviously just been a great deal more disorientated than he had first imagined.

He tried to explain this to Katrina now but she refused to listen. She had decided that the Blackhart was dangerous and he could not change her mind. But he would go for his run anyway. Deep down she had always known this, but she also knew that she had to at least *try* to stop him.

He left her looking sad and bewildered on the bed, with repeated assurances that he would be extra careful and that he would not be long. But by then he was almost frantic with excitement. He seemed to feel the forest calling out to him, reaching for him, drawing him closer and closer until he thought he would burst from the pressure. It was a new and powerful emotion and Richard was completely overcome. He revelled in it; it coursed through his body and flooded his very soul like a flow of electricity pulsing stronger with each heartbeat.

And then suddenly he was in the forest and his nerves were on fire. He had never felt so purely alive, so filled with energy and passion and sheer exhilaration. He was beyond any level of conscious thought but he *knew*, actually *knew*, beyond any shadow of doubt that the girl was waiting for him at the clearing. So he ran on towards her, filled with an indefinable ecstasy and entirely oblivious of all the eyes which watched him and all the feet which followed in his tracks.

Richard knew only that he would soon be at the clearing, and that the girl would be there too. He had no idea why he felt so compelled to see her again but his elation was so great that he could not think of anything but the girl, and of course the wonderful forest itself, which smelled so good and felt so warm and so fresh.

The creatures who followed felt it too. The forest pulled them towards him like a magnet and when he saw the girl standing still beneath the Elm exactly as he had expected he stopped short and for a moment he could barely breathe. She looked different, older somehow, and her face had replaced mischief with something darker which he did not even recognise. And once he had managed to tear his gaze away from her he finally noticed something much more important. This time she was not alone.

**

Katrina sat alone in Richard's bedroom. She was scared almost to the point of panic and dare not move lest the rising hysteria overtake her completely. Instead she hugged her knees to her chest and tried in vain to control the shivering.

It had begun about five minutes after Richard had left and she seemed powerless to stop it. Despite the warmth of the evening she had become chilled to the very core of her being and once the shaking had started she had known it would be a long time before she was able to move again. She knew this because it had happened before, only the once, thank God, but it was not something she was likely to forget and she knew that it would not stop unless she stayed still and tried to keep calm.

So she did try, but it was far from easy. Last time she had felt these tremors she had lost a sister, and now the man she loved was in danger and again she was helpless as a baby. Shaking and terrified, there was nothing she could do but wait. Just like she had waited for Bethany all those year ago. The most frightening thing of all was that she could not feel his presence anymore. Usually, with her sharp instincts, she could centre on him easily and share a little of his feelings, just like she had done last night in fact. But since he entered the Blackhart there was nothing. Unless you count the stinging pain in the middle of her forehead which appeared like a flash of lightening whenever she made an attempt to focus on him. It was as though she was being deliberately shut out for some reason, and the idea that that could be true was so sinister she could not even bear to think about it.

Instead she tried not to think at all. To empty her mind completely in the hope that her body would take the hint and relax. She had been taking yoga classes for months and had been taught that the art of meditation was "essential for both physical and mental well-being". Katrina, however, had never really taken it too seriously, and consequently she now wished she had paid more attention and could fall swiftly into the trance-like state she was supposed to be so well-practised at. Sadly, though, she wasn't well-practised at all, and the effort of trying so hard now was simply making things worse by adding to the frustration she already felt. So she just continued to hug her knees and wait for it to end. After all, if she was rational about it, there was no real basis for her fears whatsoever: Richard was a grown man, fit and strong and clever, and even if he did see the girl again, there was no reason to believe that she meant him any harm. And besides how could a mere girl possibly be capable of hurting Richard in any way?

Katrina was well aware that these arguments were sensible, logical and beyond reproach, but she also knew that they were total crap. Her entire body was screaming with fear and no amount of rational thinking was going to overcome her most basic instinct - that Richard was in trouble and that he needed to get out of the forest as quickly as possible. She felt the urgency grow once more and tried again to focus on him - but the pain was too much. It shot through her skull like an ice-tipped knife and she cried out, more from anger and frustration than from the pain itself. Why couldn't she feel him? Is this how other people felt all the time, not knowing if their loved ones were OK or not? She could not imagine living like that and wondered, as she had many times before, how anyone could get through the day without being able to centre on their family and friends for reassurance that they would be seeing them again. Katrina was used to doing this continually, and she knew she would not be able to calm herself until she could do it again - then at least she would have a vague idea of what was happening out there.

The shaking continued as Katrina waited. Her entire body ached and the pain in her head grew stronger as her fear intensified. And then everything stopped.

Suddenly, a blanket of peace surrounded her and she was able to breathe quietly and stretch out her sore, stiff limbs. She reached for Richard immediately and found only that he was alive, but still in the forest and too far away to focus on properly. She was relieved though, and glad it was over, for she felt that nothing more would happen tonight. It had been well over an hour since he left and she knew that it would take him a long time to find his way home again. But she also knew that he would come home, and she would be waiting for him.

She stood up and stamped her feet, trying to ease the horrible 'pins and needles' which had set in, but as she did so a powerful image struck her mind and she reached for the bedside phone. She quickly replaced the receiver, however, as she realised that it might seem a little strange to order an ambulance in advance. She would wait until he was nearly home, that way it should arrive just on time.

**

55

Bethany had no idea what to do. She stood and stared and waited and stared some more and finally she realised that the reason she didn't know what to do was that suddenly she was scared. In fact she was terrified. She had been so looking forward to this moment, to seeing his face when he realised what she had planned for him, but now she was just as scared as he was.

Of course, Richard wasn't actually scared of her; all he was worried about was the huge congregation of animals around her. And she could see how that could be a little threatening for someone who did not know them. But Bethany also knew that it was not the animals he should be concerned about; after all, they wouldn't start anything unless either she or the forest itself commanded it, and it was this which frightened her the most. She knew she was supposed to be in control tonight, was supposed to be doing something important to hurt and threaten the one she had dreamed of for so long. But now, somehow, she couldn't think straight, couldn't bring herself to harm the man she had once adored so much. Yet she knew it was too late for that. She could feel the forest's energy sizzling in the air and vibrating through the very ground she stood on. The Blackhart was not going to give up so easily and she was sure that in a few moments she would be as much at its mercy as the creatures who waited with her. And so she was scared, because it was hard to fight the forest, it was so much cleverer than she was, its memory was impeccable and it was stronger than anything else she had ever known. But as she waited and as she stared and as she fought the Blackhart's impatience with all her might, she also realised that for all it's power the forest was easily distracted when it came to one thing: the thrill of the chase. And after all, Richard had come here to run hadn't he? So this way everyone was happy. And if he happened to trip and hurt himself *whilst* he was running - well then that wouldn't be her fault at all.

**

The staring seemed to go on for ever and then, just as he had been preparing a desperate escape attempt, the girl snapped out of her reverie and bolted behind the elm tree. At first, the incredible array of wildlife still kept him frozen with fear, especially as he knew they surrounded the entire area, but as the sea of animals parted right in front of him he quickly understood that he was *supposed* to follow her.

Trying not to think about the crowd closing in behind him, he chased after her and seemed to glimpse only her hair as she dashed ahead, weaving effortlessly in and out of trees and shrubs like they weren't actually there at all. Or perhaps it was the girl herself who wasn't there, for at times her body seemed to melt into the scenery as if she wasn't running around the trees but directly into them, only to appear again at an impossible distance before him. The whole scene had the same dreamlike quality he had experienced before, and as twilight set in he began to notice changes in the forest which left him bewildered and increasingly uneasy.

Obviously the animals were still following, which was incredible anyway; a hoard of foxes, roe deer, badgers, weasels, even squirrels and rabbits, and others he simply did not recognise. The foxes had scared him the most, at first, with their low growling and sharp incisors bared menacingly, but then he had noticed the black boar, and the fox had paled into insignificant overgrown puppies. The boar was much bigger and looked as strong as a bull. It pawed at the ground with impatience, sharp horns swaying from side to side and bottomless black eyes holding his gaze until he was forced to look away from the murderous intent which was so clear. They all ran with him now, boar included, too close for comfort as he tried not to hear the thunderous echo of their perpetual advance. And of course the birds were with him too. A multitude of wings, all shapes and sizes, flapping and fluttering above him. He had never been much of a bird-spotter but he was sure there was at least one kestrel up there, possibly two, and quite a combination of owls and hawks, though mostly he saw magpies and blue tits and wood pigeons and some rather large woodpeckers whose beaks shone like knives in the dwindling light. Nothing made sense anymore and the more he acknowledged their continued presence the more he understood that he was in great danger tonight. Katrina had been right, as usual, and Richard was beginning to wish that for once he had taken her advice and simply stayed at home.

But instead he was here in the Blackhart, utterly lost and chasing a beautiful teenage girl and in turn *being* chased by seemingly all the animals who lived here. Surely, this could not be happening. Maybe he had stayed home after all and he had fallen asleep and this was just a crazy nightmare from which he would soon awake in his lovely new house. But he knew that was just wishful thinking. The elation he had felt earlier still hung somewhere in the background of his tormented mind and he remembered only too well how he had ended up in this situation. And there was no escape now. He could do nothing but what was intended, for the only safe place away from spiked horns, snapping jaws and vicious claws was forward and fast. So Richard ran. Faster and faster as the darkness drew in and the forest turned black and dense and monstrous. His vision faded, his fear mounted and he tripped and fell with almost every step. Huge trees blocked his path constantly, as if on purpose, and he fell into holly and brambles and thorns until his legs and arms were streaked with blood. Yet still he tried to run. The girl shimmered and skipped in the distance, always in view, always laughing, mocking his falls and showing no signs of tiring whatsoever. And despite his fear and exhaustion he still longed to reach her. She tantalised him, mesmerised him, reached out to him and pulled him on though he knew he should resist. But it was too late for that. His body was torn and aching but his mind was lost in her grip and as long as she was still in his sights he could somehow ignore the fear and force himself to follow. So he kept on running.

**

Bethany was getting tired. Just a little, but definitely tired. They were deep inside the Blackhart now and she could feel its energy pulsing all around them. Trees were stirring as the darkness settled upon them and their roots rippled and shook as Richard ran over them, causing fall after fall which cut and bruised his delicate skin until she began to fear for him again. She knew he would fall hard soon, and the running would be over, but then the creatures would be upon him and that would be the end: no more Richard Dean Haley. And she was not going to let that happen. It wasn't fair. She should be the one to decide what to do with him, not the forest, and as she slowed the pace to allow her pursuer to keep up she drew on all her strength and willed the animals to go home. "Not now," she whispered, "not yet, little ones, go home, rest, go home my friends, go home now." She felt the forest's anger and she screamed aloud "HE'S MINE!" and then she stopped and turned and he was already on the ground, the boar upon him, nostrils flaring and hooves trampling. She raced over and laid a hand upon its brow muttering softly, and it quickly backed away and charged off through the undergrowth. Richard lay still and she bent closer to him, taking his hand and scanning for injury. The boar had broken his left arm near the wrist with its stamping but other than that it was just cuts and bruises. She knew he had been very lucky and though she was relieved she had no desire to heal his arm so she rose to leave him and began to turn away. But, as she did so, she noticed his eyelids flicker and realised that he was no longer unconscious.

"Richard Dean Haley." She looked directly into his eyes and spoke his name very clearly and very slowly, as though savouring the sounds in her mouth. The man at her feet just stared, awe-struck, and she realised for the first time that he didn't remember either. So she surprised him and spoke again: "You will understand, I promise." And then she was gone.

**

Richard had lost consciousness when he heard her scream. The sound had pierced his skull and driven into every corner of his being like a cold black chisel puncturing his soul. His hands had flown instinctively up to cover his ears and at the same time he had tripped on yet another tree root and hit his head on the trunk it was attached to. He had no memory of the fall, nor, thankfully, of the harsh attentions of the black boar he had been so right to fear; all he remembered was that deafening cry which seemed to tear the very fabric of reality and then . . . nothing. He had woken to the warmth of a small hand softly holding his cold rough palm and he had been too shocked to move. He lay still and felt something peaceful and strange pass through his body and then the small hand disappeared and he dared to open his eyes.

She stood there in the moonlight, frail and exquisite like a fallen star gently shimmering above him and for a moment his fear and pain dissolved entirely. He gazed up at her, openly amazed, and when she spoke it was the sound of an angel choir blessing his name with virtue and grace. He could not answer her, he simply continued to gaze at her wondrous face until suddenly she frowned and looked steadily at him with such a shocked and knowing expression that he could not help but frown back at her. She spoke the next words much quieter, he had to strain to make them out, but he knew that he wanted to understand *right now*, and when she went it was like someone switched off all the lights, and he was left alone, lost in the forest, cold and confused, wounded and sore and, quite frankly, more afraid than he had ever though it possible to be.

10

Elan

He had no reason to be afraid now, although Bethany didn't really care to make him feel comfortable. She was tired herself, and not at all happy, and it took the last of her energy to guide him home safely, especially as it was such a long way back. She had not realised quite how deep into the forest she had taken him, and she wondered how much control she had actually had during that time. She had not meant to run so far at all, in fact she had not done anything she had planned tonight. And again she wondered why she was expending so much energy on trying to help Richard rather than trying to harm him as she had intended. Everything was so confusing to her and she couldn't think straight at all. Part of her mind was busy showing Richard the invisible pathway to the clearing and the rest of her was trying to make sense of what she had just done. Why had she saved him? Why was she helping him out of the forest even still? If she stopped now he would probably never get out alive, especially with the bitter and turbulent mood the Blackhart was in at the moment. Its rage still shook the ground now and then and the trees had not yet been calmed either, their branches swayed and creaked and she could feel the roots straining to trip him or to wrap around his legs like enraged pythons. It took the last of her powers to quell their eagerness and as she chanted she curled her body even tighter around the base of the Father Tree until slowly it allowed her to soothe and pacify its furious spirit.

The Father Tree was named as such because it was

the oldest and largest in the Forest and therefore its life-force was by far the strongest. It was a giant oak tree and over the years she had grown to love it so much she had even named it - a rare honour, only it and the old fox had been named by her - but though Elan was usually a gentle giant, tonight it raged with all the might of the Blackhart and Bethany was exhausted from her efforts.

She slept for a while, once she knew that Richard was safe, and Elan's thick boughs gave her shelter as the storm rampaged through the forest like a wild beast suddenly let loose from its chains. Bethany never knew about the storm and when she awoke all was fresh and bright and calm. She had dreamed a new dream, and she knew now what she had to do. And if she could not hurt Richard then she must at least make sure there were no other girls to take her place. No, the forest was hers and hers alone, so they must be taught to stay away. And then she would be safe again, and they would be safe too, and maybe Richard would remember and then he would go away again and everything would go back to the way it was and she wouldn't have to think anymore and hurt her head and she could just forget about *all* of it.

Bethany felt sick. Her head throbbed and her mouth was dry and she just wanted to rest some more but she knew they would be walking to school soon and she knew she must go through with her plan this time and do it properly - for that was the only way to end it all, for ever.

11

After the run

Katrina had called for the ambulance already and was expecting Richard's return at any moment. Unusually, though, she did not feel too exact about the timing so she just had to hope that he would arrive before the sirens or she would have some tricky explaining to do. She was really too worried to care though, especially as she felt that Richard was already on the verge of collapse, so the ambulance needed to be here as soon as possible.

She did not have long to wait. She watched him limp through the garden, one arm cradling the other, and she hurried to the back door to help him inside. She heard the sirens then, and could not help but smile - her timing had been impeccable after all - but then she looked properly at her injured man and the smile soon disappeared. He shivered and shook uncontrollably and reminded her of the state she had been in when he first left. But this was much worse. He was freezing cold and covered head to foot in scratches and dried blood. His broken arm looked crooked and swollen and his T-shirt and shorts were ripped and muddied, leaves and twigs still stuck in the cotton as well as in his hair. She tenderly lay the ready blanket over his shoulders and wrapped it around him. He was clearly in a state of severe shock and exhaustion, and she wasn't sure how much longer he would stay conscious. If only he had listened to her! But she was too concerned to be angry now, and besides, what good would it do to say 'I told you so'? It certainly wouldn't mend his tattered body or soothe his tortured spirit. So she said nothing. She kissed the top of his head gently and went to answer the door. He had passed out by the time they got to him, and they had to carry him on a stretcher with all the nosy neighbours peering through their curtains. Katrina pretended not to see them and went in the ambulance with him. She held his hand throughout the journey and tried in vain to block out the powerful sensation of her sister which had bombarded her senses from the moment she had touched him. She still wasn't sure if she believed in ghosts but now there was one thing she was definitely sure of: the girl he had seen in the forest was her sister, and somehow, for some strange reason, she had also held his hand tonight.

**

Richard awoke the next day in a starched, uncomfortable hospital bed with absolutely no recollection of how he had got there or why. The lower half of his left arm was already in a cast and he was aching absolutely everywhere but other than that he felt surprisingly well and his first thought was that the girl had spoken to him last night. He tried to piece together the evening's events but the only part which wasn't blurred was the vision of a shimmering angel standing above him and speaking his name. He knew she had said something else too, something more important, but he couldn't concentrate with the image of her face so bright in his mind. She seemed to shine behind his eyes and hypnotise his thoughts in such a way that he quickly lost touch of whether he was sleeping or not, until all he knew was the girl and her exquisite voice repeating his name over and over and over...

"Richard? ... Richard? ..."

She touched his face lightly and the spell broke as he opened his eyes. She smiled at him shyly and a flash of recognition passed through him so quickly he instantly forgot it had happened and he saw only Katrina, the woman he loved and had let down.

"I'm so sorry baby, I should've listened to you, I don't know what to say." He looked so miserable suddenly that she was lost for words too and she simply leant over to hold him so he would understand that she couldn't possible be angry.

"It's OK hon." She kissed him and held on to his hand like she would never let go, "You're OK and that's all that really matters isn't it? I just want to get you home now and we can talk when you feel a bit more alive."

"I'm fine," he answered far too fast, "and there's nothing to talk about anyway. I guess I just got lost and fell over in the dark or something. I don't really remember."

She looked at him and rolled her eyes. "This is me, hon, so don't give me that crap. Besides, I know who she is, and there's something I ha.."

But he cut her off rudely, frantic with excitement. "You know?! You know who she is? You... how... Oh my God are you serious? You mean we can go and see her and find out what's going on and.."

"Enough." Katrina managed to say the word quietly but with more force than if she had shouted at the top of her voice. She pulled the curtains around the bed and emptied a carrier bag of clothes on top of the sheets, all the time holding his gaze steadily until she could see that he had calmed down.

"I need to get you home," she continued, firm but just as quiet, "and first and foremost you need to rest. And that's not negotiable. I won't tell you a bloody thing unless you calm down and do as your told for once in your life, OK?"

Richard sulked like a schoolboy but managed to

mumble "OK" as he swung his legs over the side of the bed and began to dress. Katrina had to help him with almost everything and he began to realise how hard it was going to be to function with only one arm, and with the rest of him feeling like he'd just been run over by a truck. He did not recall ever feeling so stiff and ungainly and he knew that the next few days would be dreadful for both of them as he learnt what he could and could not do on his own. Yet he still wanted to find the girl, and if Katrina knew who she was then surely he could just go to her house and the whole thing with the forest could be forgotten.

"Well, can't you at least tell me her name?" He ventured, breaking the silence and using his most plaintive expression. "Please?"

She looked down and tied the laces on his trainers, hoping he wouldn't see the tears pricking at the corners of her eyes. God, she thought, I'm just a big cry-baby at the moment, what the Hell's the matter with me? She swallowed hard and took a deep breath. "Her name is Bethany", she said at last, "at least I'm fairly certain it is. But there is a way to know for certain." She reached into her handbag and took a small picture from her wallet. She glanced at it momentarily before thrusting it into Richard's hands and turning to sit beside him as he looked in pure amazement at the photograph he held.

"Where did you get this? How . . . who is she?"

"So it is her. I wasn't sure if I really believed it. Are you absolutely positive hon? Is this really the girl you saw?" She managed to look distressed, disturbed and hopeful all at once.

"Yes, of course it is, I'd recognise that smile anywhere. You said her name was Bethany, right? Is she a friend of yours? Do you know her last name?"

Katrina finally let the tears run down he cheeks as she answered him, "Yes, I know her last name. It's

67

Rose. Bethany Rose. She's my sister."

12

Katz

Katherine Isabelle Katson (Katie K to her mum, Katherine to her dad, and Katz to herself and everyone else) was walking to school on her own that morning as her best friend Trudy was off sick with yet another dose of tonsillitis. She got throat infections constantly so Katz was quite used to walking alone, and besides, it was a beautiful spring morning for the forest shortcut. Hundreds of bluebells bathed the ground on either side of the pathway and the sun shone through the trees in golden streaks, making them flicker and flare in the warm swaying breeze.

She walked lazily, dreamily, enjoying the fresh scent of the forest and all it's lively colours and sounds. The birds sang happily and she felt like whistling along with them (which of course she would never do, it just wouldn't be *cool*) and she grinned to herself instead as she thought of her new teacher, Mr Haley, who would take her first class of the day - English Literature. Katz had always been good at English classes but had never really shown any particular interest in them until now. Until Mr Haley, with his amazing blue eyes under those wonderful dark eyebrows, with his unbelievably sexy half-smile and that wonderful fit body which she could tell just rippled with muscle under his oh so cool designer shirts.

She knew it was just a dream, a teenage crush on an older man who was completely inaccessible. She was far too switched on to be kidding herself that it was true love or anything like she had heard some of the other girls suggest. Because of course it was all over the school by now. Every girl (and even some of the boys she had noticed, amused) was 'madly in love' with the new teacher after just one day and he had been the main topic of discussion at every opportunity, including many phone calls in the evening until her parents had finally confiscated her mobile in exasperation.

But although it was just a crush, and nothing could possibly happen between them, Katz didn't see what was wrong with looking as good as possible for school today. She had done the best she could with the boring uniform - last years skirt which was just a fraction too short and too tight, and one extra button left open on her shirt. She knew she had very little yet in the way of cleavage but as she had recently started wearing bras she figured it was worth a try. And then, of course, there was the perfume she had 'borrowed' from her mum and the make-up she had put on with a small compact mirror (also 'borrowed' from mum) whilst leaning against a tree the moment she had left the street and entered the Blackhart.

Katz's mother was quite strict compared to some of her friends' mums, and at thirteen she was not yet allowed to wear make-up except on very special occasions - such occasions to be determined by her parents and not herself of course. So although a few of her friends wore make-up for school all the time, this would be a first for her and she was actually a tiny bit nervous. Mainly because if her mum found out she would be totally crucified but also because Trudy wasn't there to ask if she looked OK. In fairness, she was well aware that she looked OK. She knew she was lucky enough to have been born with good cheekbones and big brown eyes and long curly eyelashes which even Trudy envied. She had long, strawberry blonde hair, straight but thick so it bounced and shone in the sun, and her lips were full and expressive. Her mother had told her that the main reason she didn't want her wearing make-up was because, apparently, her skin was so perfect that foundation would ruin it, and she had decided that this was probably true - her skin was soft and pure all over and she hadn't used any foundation today for she didn't want to spoil her already flawless complexion.

So she didn't really need Trudy to tell her that she looked OK. But what she wanted was to be told she looked much better than that. The words she would have loved to hear were more along the lines of: "stunning, beautiful, gorgeous", or even just "sexy as Hell"! And it wasn't really Trudy she wanted to hear them from, it was Mr. Haley. In her dream he would ask her to stay behind after class and then he would lock the door and take her by the hand. He would gaze longingly into her eyes and as he leaned forward to kiss her he would murmur softly how beautiful she was and...

Katz jumped and let out a small cry as a fox shot across the path in front of her. She stopped walking and laughed at her surprise but before she could continue a rustle of leaves from behind stopped her again and she turned slowly, heart thumping, as a hazy figure appeared in the distance. Then she breathed out heavily in relief and the last thing she remembered was that she was incredibly happy and incredibly safe and suddenly incredibly, incredibly sleepy.

**

She was found the following day, at around 5.45 am. Jeremy Katson, Katherine's father, had not slept at all and had gone out to look for her again, retracing her footsteps on the path to school which had taken her somewhere else instead. And as he walked the same path he had trailed up and down so many times the day before, he noticed her body on a bed of ferns which looked bizarrely as though they had been deliberately placed to cushion her sleeping body. At first he only recognised the uniform and her much adored Nike sports bag, but as he looked closer he was forced to admit that the distorted mass of flesh on her face really did belong to his beautiful Katherine, for she wore the delicate diamond earrings he had bought her for her first birthday as a teenager, and the matching necklace she had pestered him for a week later. But now the beautiful face was no more, and as he stared in horror at the mangled scar tissue which replaced it his knees finally gave way and he fell to the floor beside her, convulsing with sorrow and outrage and utter incomprehension. His daughter, confused and groggy, woke to the sound of her father's hysteria and was immediately terrified at the sight of the only man she truly adored in such uncontrollable anguish.

"Dad?" Her voice was scratchy and dry, too quiet. "Daddy?" She still sounded scratchy, but much louder. "You're really scaring me Daddy. What's wrong? Where are we?" She sat up then and soon realised that she was still in the forest, but it didn't seem like morning anymore; it was dark and cold and she worried that she had fallen asleep and slept all day and that's why her father was so distressed.

"Daddy, I'm fine, I'm sorry, I don't know what happened but I'm fine, honestly." She pleaded with him and eventually he gathered his senses and stood up to hold her. He was ashamed of it, but he could not bring himself to look at her face so he wrapped his coat around her shoulders and walked at her side holding her tight against him and trying hard to stifle his choking sobs.

He knew Katherine was scared by his reaction but he could not control his shock and he also knew that the worst was yet to come. Her mother would be waiting, both frantic and numbed, and then there was the mirror in the hallway. He tried to think of comforting words but nothing came to mind and when they reached the house there was just the screaming, and the screaming, and the screaming.

Jeremy Katson had found his daughter, but he had lost his little girl for ever.

**

Hartsbridge was a small town so it wasn't long before Katherine's fate hit the headlines of the local Gazette. Katrina had heard stories on the grapevine of course but she had been careful not to mention anything to Richard as his mind was still reeling from the events of Monday night, and from the revelations which followed. He had listened intently as she explained the circumstances of her sister's disappearance but he refused point blank to believe that he had seen a ghost. He simply did not believe in ghosts and that was that. So his brain was working overtime to try and arrive at a more rational conclusion which he would be able to cope with. As yet, the best he could do was that the girl in the forest wasn't actually Bethany at all, she just happened, by some alarming coincidence, to look exactly like her - presumably right down to the specific positioning of moles and freckles on her arms and neck. It was, in Katrina's opinion, a pretty poor hypothesis but, as she didn't believe her sister was dead either, she couldn't exactly argue with him - after all, how can you see the ghost of someone who's still alive?

So they were both confused, and Richard was still very tired and pale and she didn't want to add to his troubles by telling him that one of his pupils had been horribly mutilated beyond recognition. The police, however, just wanted to catch the madman who had done such a dreadful thing, so the fact that she had hidden the newspaper under a pile of magazines became suddenly irrelevant.

No. 2, Blackhart Drive must have been the first call of the day for it was five to nine in the morning when Katrina answered the knock. She had temporarily moved in to Richard's house so that she could take care of him and she was being overly strict in a way which both charmed and annoyed him to varying degrees. When the police arrived, he was laid out on the sofa under an old coffee-stained blanket which looked like it had been stolen from the previous century, and because he was probably the only person in Hartsbridge not to know about Katherine, he was more than a little surprised to see them.

He sat up quickly and tried to hide the awful blanket behind him but as they explained the reason behind the visit he soon forgot to be embarrassed and could only listen wide-eyed as the constable advised him that there had been an "incident" in the forest the previous day involving one of the girls in his English Literature class. They were "not at liberty to reveal any names or details at this time" but were going door to door in the surrounding neighbourhood to find out if anyone had seen or heard anything unusual at the time of the incident.

The two policemen, DC Hobbs and DC Barlow, CID, were extremely thorough with their questioning and despite the fact that both Richard and Katrina had been in Harts Hospital until 9.30 am on the day it happened they still felt like they were being treated as suspects in the strange case. Apparently, because "the young girl in question" had no memory of the incident itself they had no specific time-frame to work on, which meant that the crime could have been committed at any time between approximately eight a.m. and twelve noon, which was apparently when her father first entered the forest to look for her.

They asked a seemingly endless amount of questions about Richard's new job and the reasons behind his move from central London to a small town in the North, as if they simply could not understand why anyone would want to leave a good career in a large city school to come *here*, of all places. They also asked them both about Richard's own particular incident in the forest, and though they glanced at each other from time to time, neither felt it necessary to mention the girl he had chased, or the fact that, impossibly, hundreds of animals had gathered to chase him too. Katrina was sure that the younger policeman, Hobbs, knew they were hiding something, but DC Barlow, clearly the man in charge, cut him short several times and seemed to be in a hurry to leave, probably aware that they had another twenty doors to knock on before they could go home.

When they did leave, finally, Katrina rushed straight to the kitchen and retrieved the Gazette as hastily as she had hidden it. They read it together and, like all the other Hartsbridge residents, tried and failed to understand what had happened to poor Katherine Katson two days ago.

"I don't get this. It says she's been scarred but she wasn't actually hurt. What the Hell does that mean? You don't get scars in a day. I mean, am I reading this wrong? Am I missing something?" Richard kept flicking the page over and back, searching for an answer.

"No. I don't get it either." Katrina had read the whole article and knew there was no answer. "I know who she is though. The paper isn't allowed to give names if they're under eighteen but it's been all over

75

town since yesterday. Apparently she thought she was fine until she got home and saw her face in the mirror - and then they reckon you could hear her screaming three streets away. Poor kid."

"You mean you knew about this?" Richard looked at her, astonished and extremely annoyed. "Why didn't you tell me? For God's sake Kate this is important."

"I'm sorry," she snapped back, clearly not sorry at all, "I didn't want to worry you. And don't call me Kate, you know I hate it."

"Whatever," he couldn't be bothered to fight. "Anyway, who is the poor girl then? They said she was in my Lit class but I don't really know them yet, I mean I was only there for one bloody day and then all this crap started."

Richard rubbed his cast absent-mindedly and Katrina sighed; she didn't want to fight either.

"Her name is Katherine Katson." She paused as he tried to put a face to the name. "Lives on Wicker Grove, you know the one with the big old Victorian houses? It's only a couple of streets down from my place. I remember her when she was little. Pretty blonde rich kid, spoilt rotten by her dad with all the designer gear, you know the type."

"Oh my God, I know the one. Long hair, quite grown up for her age. She told me to call her 'Katz - with a 'z' not an 's' '. First thing she said," he smiled at the sudden recollection, "made me laugh actually."

"Well I don't think she'll be making you laugh anymore, that's for sure." Katrina sipped on her fourth cup of coffee and relayed all the gossip she had previously kept from him. "Jen knows all about it 'cos. her bastard boyfriend's brother lives next door to them. Apparently she's suicidal so they're keeping her sedated and she never leaves her room. And the only person who's been allowed to see her except her

76

parents is some fancy plastic surgeon but they don't think he can do anything. That's how bad it is."

"God. Poor kid." Richard looked genuinely upset as he tried to imagine how someone's face could be "scarred beyond recognition" as the journalist had worded it. He pictured the bright teenager who wanted to be called Katz "with a 'z'" and could not conceive of such a pretty young face being so permanently ruined.

"Surely she must remember something? And I still don't get this scarring thing. I mean, if you take it literally they're asking us to believe that without her ever feeling a thing she was somehow abducted and then taken somewhere and had her face cut to ribbons and then miraculously it just healed completely - all in the space of twenty four hours!" His expression was utter incredulity as he scanned the article yet again. "In fact, less than that, look, she was found 'in the early hours of Tuesday morning'!" He flung the paper across the room in disgust and looked at Katrina as though expecting an explanation.

"Don't look at me!" She replied, aghast. "I don't get it any more than you do. It makes about as much sense as you chasing my fifteen year old sister all around the forest *three days ago* when the last time I saw her, also aged fifteen, was fourteen bloody years ago!"

She hitched her breath as a sob stuck in her throat and Richard drew her close to him. Over the last few days he had seen a soft side to Katrina that he never would have believed existed, and he knew she was still deeply traumatised over Bethany's disappearance. So, for the moment he tried not to think of Katherine or of the barefooted girl or of anything at all; he just held her tight and kissed her tears away and hoped he wasn't lying when he told her that everything would be OK.

13

Zoe

For the rest of the week, Richard seemed to be right: everything was, well, as OK as it could be under the circumstances. Yellow tape cut off access to the forest path from either side and PCs scoured the area for the tiniest of clues, but for everyone else life went on as it always does after a tragedy - with a bizarre and unfeeling normality, because life can't just stop, no matter how much people may want it to. Of course the PCs soon became bored and despondent with their tedious and fruitless activities, and after a while people stopped talking about poor Katherine and got on with their lives. The only major difference was that for the time being nobody else was allowed into the forest, not that anyone particularly wanted to go there, but it meant that the shortcut to Blackleigh Comprehensive was out-of-bounds, so children were either driven to and from school or were forced to walk the extra mile through the streets.

By the following week, however, Richard was back at work and was again the main topic of discussion in the school yard. His cast was soon covered in scrawled jokes and signatures and only Katherine's closest friends still showed any signs of distress. The initial panic had died down all too quickly, and although the yellow tape still hung across the Blackhart's entrances, the PCs had given up their search and no self-respecting teenager was going to be stopped by a small piece of yellow tape. So the path was used once more. No-one mentioned it to their parents of course, but the weather was fine and the path was just more convenient and besides, it had been a week now and nothing else had happened so it must be OK. Their logic was the simple rational of all young teenagers: bad things only happen to other people. Still, at first they stayed in groups, all wary though they would never admit it, but fairly soon they forgot to be cautious; after all, they had used the forest path since they were kids, and it was hard to stay scared of something which was so familiar.

Which was why none of them really noticed when Zoe Anne Bishop bent down to tie her shoelaces and dropped her bag on the floor, spilling its contents into a small ditch at the side of the path. She shouted to her friends to "hold up a minute" but they were both plugged into the same iPhone, sharing the new Olly Murs track. Kelly found the phone in one of her brother's favourite hiding places - inside his stereo speaker. She had found all sorts of things in there and he was so stupid he still had no idea that she knew about it. The problem was that he had too many hiding places, so when he couldn't find something where he thought he'd left it, he had to check about a dozen other locations, by which time of course his little sister had put it back and he was none the wiser.

Anyway, with Olly Murs at full volume they didn't hear Zoe asking them to wait, and as she fumbled in the ditch for her precious iPod and a few scruffy school books they rounded a corner up ahead and she was left completely alone, muttering "oh bollocks" under her breath as she searched frantically for her favourite pink headphones.

She found them later, they were already in her hand when she woke up, but by then it was very dark and she was freezing and scared and her left eye wouldn't open properly and she just wanted to go home. Crying and confused, she ran down the path and out of the Blackhart, trying but failing miserably to remember how she had come to be sleeping in the forest. And as she wiped her tears away she began to scream, for the face she had just touched couldn't possibly be hers, so knotted and rough, and she knew then that bad things didn't just happen to other people and she wasn't immortal after all.

Zoe's mum and brother heard her screams before they saw her and when the doctor arrived he had to sedate all three of them.

**

The only other person to see Zoe Bishop that night was Katrina, and she really wished she hadn't. She had not been sleeping well of late and at two a.m. had decided that enough was enough so she left Richard snoring in bed and went downstairs to make coffee. At least, that would be her excuse if he woke up, because what she really needed was a cigarette, and though she had quit smoking over three years ago when the craving occasionally reappeared she was far to weak to overcome it. It took her a while to find the emergency pack she kept in her handbag as she seemed to keep a hundred other emergency items in there as well: nail files, make-up, inhaler, pills for every possible ailment, and an assortment of diaries, note books and crumpled bits of paper with hastily written phone numbers and messages from people she couldn't even remember. In short, it was chaos in there and of course the squashed packet was right at the bottom now that she only smoked around one cigarette every six to eight months.

But she did find it eventually and, dressed only in pyjamas and flip-flops, she slipped quietly out of the door and perched uncomfortably on the wall surrounding Richard's front garden. She smoked slowly, savouring the forbidden taste and the dizzy head-rush which accompanied it. As usual, about half way through she began to feel sick and was instantly glad she had stopped smoking, wondering for the umpteenth time how she had ever been able to smoke thirty of these disgusting things every single day for over ten years.

She stubbed it out on the floor so as not to leave a mark on Richard's wall - he was bound to notice - and also wondered why she was being so considerate for a change when normally she would have laughed at his obsessive cleanliness and probably left the butt sitting on top of his precious wall too. But she realised that recently her feelings had been altering towards him and incredibly she hadn't even thought of being with another man since she had come here on that first Sunday and had ended up never going home again. It was a completely new feeling she was experiencing, but it was not unpleasant, and as she pondered this new awakening in her love-life the sound of someone running broke her reverie and she looked up, startled.

There was a young girl sprinting aimlessly down the hill towards her, school-clothes crumpled and covered in bracken and twigs. She passed right by Katrina on the other side of the road, totally oblivious to her stares, and she watched with more than pity as her hands touched her face momentarily and she began to scream, high pitched and keening like a wild animal trapped in metal jaws. Katrina had seen her face by the light of the street lamp and instantly wished that she had not put out the cigarette. She had never seen anything like that in her life. Where her face should have been was instead a mass of flesh, her nose just a single small opening and only one eye visible beneath the spaghetti-like scar tissue which had replaced her forehead. Her lips were twisted, obscene, and bulged offensively over the grim distortion of skin which had once been a perfectly dimpled chin. Katrina inhaled sharply and bowed her head in horror as she hurried back into the house. The girl was obviously racing home and she was ashamed of the selfish hope building inside her that the house she was racing to was too far away for her to hear the screams of her family which would surely greet her. She wanted another cigarette just then, in fact she wanted to smoke until she puked, but her fear of going back outside was even stronger that the compulsion for nicotine. Instead she wandered into the living room in search of a stronger drink than coffee, but suddenly she felt strangely drawn to the window where she had no option but to pull back the edge of the curtain and look out into the night. She stared hard at the distant trees of the forest which she hated so much and as she silently cursed its name her whole body broke out in goose pimples and she shivered, suddenly terrified for no apparent reason. Her hand released the curtain as if it was on fire and she stepped backwards, chest heaving, until, just as suddenly, the moment passed and she could breathe again. She reached into her handbag for her trusty inhaler and forced herself to calm down. It was the middle of the night, and she knew she should simply go back to bed but the fear had not left her and she knew there would be no sleep for her to find there.

So Katrina poured herself a brandy and settled on the settee with Richard's tatty blanket and a small black kitten. She switched on the TV and tried to watch a documentary on the survivors of shark attacks. At any other time she was sure she would have found it quite fascinating but tonight she could not focus on anything but the forest, always the forest, where her sister ran through impossible scenery to tease her boyfriend; where animals ignored the laws of nature and chased a man in groups of predator and prey; and where a monster now lurked, ready to cut and scar and horrify. Every bone in her body told Katrina that the forest was an evil place, but she believed just as strongly that somehow her sister was alive there, and she wanted so much to see her again, to say she was sorry, to say 'I love you'. But it was not to be. She had not set foot inside the Blackhart all her life, and now that she had seen first hand the horror it had borne her fear had intensified and she knew that the reunion she had dreamt of for fourteen years would remain forever as a dream.

Katrina slept that night after all, curled up with Frankie on the settee, brandy glass dropped empty on the floor. And she dreamed of her family: her mum and dad alive again and back in love, and Bethany holding her hand as they picked bluebells in a warm safe forest while the sun shone down upon them and the birds whistled happily in the trees.

14

Scarring & Healing

Deep in the forest even the owls were quiet tonight and Bethany slept deeply in her underground den, exhausted from her day of healing. It was hard work to cleanse and repair such damaged features but as before she had done the best she could and was thankful that her powers had held out long enough for her to finish while the girl still slept. But the strength of such magic took its toll on her frail body and she had collapsed in agony on returning to her bed that evening. Her hands hung heavy at her sides, throbbing and cramping simultaneously, and her head felt huge and swollen, ready to burst like an overripe tomato at the slightest touch. The old fox, whom she had called Chaver, was curled up on the soft bracken she had used to line her den and he instantly moved to greet her, licking her fragile fingers tenderly and nuzzling against her as she fell awkwardly onto the soft mound of hay and feathers which was her bed. She managed to speak his name softly before she passed out and so he stayed with her that night, nestled close to her back and sharing his warmth as he felt her body grow gradually colder, inwardly struggling to replenish itself.

For three days and nights she slept like that, with Chaver leaving her side only to hunt and to mark his territory well away from her home, as he knew she hated his pungent scent and he was anxious not to displease her. In his own way he was worried about his strange friend and could not understand why she did not wake, but he sensed somehow that she should not be alone and so he waited patiently each day, trusting that she would soon rise up and play with him as she had always done.

Eventually, Bethany did wake up, but though she was extremely glad of his soothing company, she was still too weak to play with the old fox, and he soon began to leave her for longer periods to return to his earth and to the shy young vixen who had recently arrived in the copse where he lived. Of course, Bethany did not mind him leaving at all, it was the way of nature and the way things should be, but in her diminished state she began to feel a loneliness she had never experienced before, a deep and powerful yearning for the comfort of her own kind which she knew she would never encounter again.

And this was only the beginning. For she knew she must recover her powers quickly, in time for the next scarring, and the next, and each time would be harder than the last until she wondered what would become of her; alone in the forest, fading and vulnerable, while the world outside could not even conceive of her existence. Except maybe for Katrina. Katrina who she felt as a burning ember in the depths of her heart, Katrina whose name she had remembered when all others had been lost, Katrina who had yelled in fury and sent her, hurting and sodden with tears, to be reborn in the forest with blood and grief and fear.

But she would not think of that now. As long as her sister's life-force still glowed within her there was hope, and she would never let go of that. She knew that Richard would return soon and there would be only two more girls to save so when his memory was restored it would be over, and if she could just conserve a little strength after so much work then she could call out to Katrina and maybe, just maybe, she would have stopped hating her by now, and maybe she would be able to see her again so she could tell her she was sorry, and tell her 'I love you'.

So Bethany slept and rested and slept some more, until slowly her powers were replenished and she felt strong and well again. But each time she slept she dreamed of Katrina, and of a new and wonderful day when they strolled through the forest hand in hand, picking bluebells while the sun shone down and the birds whistled happily in the trees.

**

Richard was worried. He was worried about Katrina, he was worried about the two damaged girls, he was worried about the morbid atmosphere in school, but most of all he was worried about the barefooted girl and, bizarrely, he was worried about the forest. He hated the fact that he could no longer run there, and he hated the fact that everyone seemed to be blaming the Blackhart itself for the scarrings, as if the very trees within it had risen up and caused the irreparable damage which everyone was now so terrified of. He just couldn't understand it. The police had spoken to the entire town, it appeared, and were scouring the undergrowth by the pathway yet again, but from what he could gather from the newspaper reports and from general rumours, they still had no leads whatsoever; no clues, no bits of hair for DNA sampling, no witnesses, no sudden memories from the victims. And the finest minds of the medical profession still had no concept of how the scarrings were even vaguely possible - they were, in fact, completely *im*possible - so of course it was easy for everyone to conjure up witches and aliens and even evil trees. But Richard refused to believe in any of that. He still loved the forest and hated that its reputation was being soiled with such nonsense. It was a beautiful place, a place of nature and freedom, and it should not be blamed for the evils of mankind just because a bad thing had happened there, twice.

Obviously, what Richard hated the most was that he was terrified of the forest as well. A place which he had loved all his life, a place he had played in, laughed in, made love in, was suddenly unsafe and intimidating. His cast was a constant, unwelcome reminder of a night he could not explain and did not want to believe in. Yet it had happened, and he still shivered at the memory with both fear and excitement; he longed to see the girl again, but feared the darkness and the glare of the wild boar which had lived on in his nightmares ever since.

So the days dragged on. At school nobody smiled much and nobody could concentrate, and at home Katrina sat and brooded, not leaving the house, barely sleeping and barely eating. She seemed to subsist entirely on coffee, brandy and cigarettes, which she thought he was unaware of, and she spent too many nights downstairs, weeping softly when she thought he was asleep. But in truth Richard wasn't sleeping much either, he was far too worried about Katrina not sleeping, but when he tried to talk to her she just shut him out even more, so he had given up, and simply held her close when she finally did come up to bed and hoped she realised that he was there for her, that he always would be.

Finally, after a week which seemed never-ending, the weekend arrived and Richard could bear it no longer. While Katrina sat smoking on the garden wall he quickly phoned her friend Jennifer and she agreed to take her out shopping for the day in Shenton, the nearest city, which he hoped would be far enough away to take her mind off both her sister and poor Zoe Bishop's face, the sight of which had clearly upset her more than she dared to admit. It would also mean, however, that he would be free to do something which he knew she would absolutely forbid, and with her 'instincts', as she called them, he figured he had a much better chance of doing it without her knowledge if she was a good few miles away at the time. He had decided to go into the forest again.

He was still more than a little scared at the prospect, but he was determined to go through with it. The police had once again given up their pointless searching and though this time they had left behind a couple of PCs to patrol the pathway he knew of various routes to the clearing which would lead right past them without being noticed. For it was back to the clearing he had to go. Back to the spot where she would appear to him as she always did, only this time he would not let her run away, not until she had told him who she was and how she knew his name, and why she looked so much like his girlfriend's little sister, and who was the monster responsible for the scarrings. For some inexplicable reason he felt she must have the answers to everything, or maybe he just *wanted* her to have all the answers, because deep down he could not understand why she would know anything at all. But she had told him he would understand hadn't she? He remembered her smooth, crystalline tone and the sparkling glow which had seemed to surround her - surely a trick of the moonlight through the trees - and his pulse began to race. She must know something, he thought, or she would not have made that promise, and that means she must also want me to go back and find her again, so that she can talk to me, so that she can tell me whatever it is I need to understand.

He kissed Katrina goodbye, trying hard not to notice how pale and tense she looked, and waited until Jen's car was safely out of sight before rushing upstairs to change. He was more interested in seeing the girl than in going for a run but he thought he had better be appropriately dressed just in case he was spotted by one of the PCs, or even just to ward of suspicious neighbours. He couldn't really run properly anyway, with his arm bouncing about painfully in its sling, but he could try a light jog and he felt the exercise would do him good after nearly two weeks of 'rest' - which as far as he could tell was merely a polite word for boredom and frustration. He paused only once as he reached the bottom of garden, briefly unwilling to pass through the gate, but he somehow managed to overcome the feeling of dread which had risen like poisonous bile in his throat and he padded steadily onwards, ducking immediately sideways at the forest entrance to avoid detection. His heart beat a solid rhythm in his chest and rang loudly in his ears like a tolling bell, but he forced himself forwards through the trees and offered a silent thank you for the early hour and the brightness of the sun. His light jog became a slow run as a surge of adrenaline dispelled any pain in his injured arm and as he ran he began to wonder what all the worry was about - the forest felt clean and true and tame, birds twittering harmlessly and a myriad of spring flowers releasing their sweet scent upon the waiting breeze. He inhaled deeply, letting the freshness flood his senses and invigorate his mind until suddenly the fear was just a figment of his past, unfettered and unnecessary, and he simply ran, at peace in the lush green sanctuary of familiar surroundings.

It took longer than usual to reach the clearing, partly because the discreet route he had taken was less direct, and partly because he was unable to match his usual pace - due mainly to being out of practise but also due to being slightly uncomfortable with a cast and a sling to slow him down. He was unusually breathless when he arrived and he paced the ground for a moment to ease his heaving chest before he realised that for once there was no-one there awaiting his arrival.

He looked around helplessly and walked a little further beyond the looming Elm which she liked to lean on, but the forest was deserted.

He was alone and annoyed, still reeling with anticipation and reluctant to leave without the climax he had been expecting. But he was also beginning to wonder if maybe the girl didn't actually exist. Maybe he had imagined the whole thing and his excuse to the hospital and to the police and to everyone but Katrina was really the truth - he had stupidly gone running in the forest after dark and had got lost, and had tripped over and bashed his arm against a tree and it was that simple. Except that didn't explain the first time he saw her, or how she just happened to be the spitting image of Katrina's long lost sister, or how he heard her speak and how he knew he couldn't possibly have imagined any of it unless he was going stark raving mad and if that was the case then they had better come and take him away quick because he *knew* it was all true.

So he would wait for a while. It was a lovely day and he had nothing better to do, well, nothing that couldn't be put off until tomorrow, so he would just sit here and wait for a while, and maybe she would come and find him for a change.

Richard settled down to wait on an old weather-smoothed tree stump and had no idea of the turmoil he was causing. Katrina may have been miles away but she was well aware of his movements and had already been sick twice at the thought of him being in the Blackhart again. She wasn't terrified like she had been the last time, but she was extremely upset at the risk he had taken and at the deliberate attempt to deceive her by making sure she was too far away to stop him. She was not sure what was in store for him today, she was tired and her instincts felt cloudy and unreliable, but she could feel them both in the forest, her sister and her lover, and all she knew was that something was very wrong with that, that neither of them was safe, that neither of them was happy.

So Katrina waited too, waited for a new instinct to arrive, a new message that would tell her what was going on, what she should do. And as she waited she shopped and talked to Jen and shopped some more, no longer even realising that she had no idea what she was buying or what she was saying, until eventually Jennifer led her to a sweet smelling cafe and let her sit and drink and smoke and cry. She had no idea what Katrina was so upset about and she knew her well enough to know that she would not talk until she was ready, so she just sat and held her hand and said all the right things until she seemed suddenly to snap upright and listen intently for something no-one else could hear.

"We have to go back now." It was a statement, not a question, and Jen was a good friend so they went back to Hartsbridge and she saw Katrina smile for the first time that day when Richard opened the door and she fell into his arms with open relief. They both waved her off from the doorstep and to anyone watching they were just like any other normal, happy couple; a little tired perhaps, but unless you were near enough to look into their eyes you would never guess how close to the edge of sanity they both were, how their insides writhed in torment while they waved and smiled and held each other far too tight.

When the moment ended they managed to break away from each other for just long enough to reach the sofa, where they hugged some more and then kissed and then finally broke the silence. It seemed a long time since they had talked properly to each other and the words sounded strange and considerably overdue.

"So what happened today?" Katrina was only mildly angry now, but she knew if he lied to her she would be fuming in an instant.

"I went for a run - in the forest." He had the good sense to seem ashamed and stared at his feet like a naughty child, "I know no-one's supposed to go in there at the moment but this whole thing's driving me batshit," he looked up at her beseechingly, "I really am sorry, I should've told you," he looked down again, "but I didn't want you to get all upset again and, well, I just *had* to go." Richard squeezed her hand and looked back at her face, "Can you understand?"

She held his gaze and nodded grudgingly, "I was just so worried. I couldn't focus properly but I knew you were in that awful place and yet I couldn't *feel* you." She sighed heavily at his confused expression and tried to explain. "I know you don't really believe in my instincts but they are real to me, and it's very scary for me when they don't seem to be working properly, and when you're in that bastard forest I just can't get a proper fix on you, and it's really freaky, and .."

He cut her off gently by putting his fingers to her lips and drawing her close again. "You're right, hon, I don't really get it, but it doesn't really matter 'cause it's something that *you* believe in, and the last thing I want is for you to be scared all day long just 'cause you're not sure if I'm OK." He brushed a stray strand of hair away from her face and looked straight into her eyes, "So, if it's that important to you, then next time I'll take my mobile, so if you need to get 'a fix' on me you can just call me, OK?" He waited for confirmation but she simply stared at him in disbelief, "OK hon? ... Katrina?"

She seemed to stare at him for quite some time until eventually she covered her face in her hands and shook her head, as if to rearrange the jumbled thoughts that

92

bounced in her brain. Richard quickly realised his mistake but he was determined not to lie to her again so he knew he would have to make her understand instead.

"Katrina, I'm sorry but I have to go back." He paused for a response but she kept on shaking her head and refused to look at him, "Don't you see I have to find her. She knows something; something important, I'm sure of it. Maybe she even knows what's going on with this scarring stuff, I don't know, but she knew my name, hon, she spoke to me like, like, oh I don't know it was just all so intense and I can't just forget about it." Richard looked down at his feet again, anxious for his girlfriend's approval, but simultaneously depressed because he knew deep down that she would never give it. Katrina also looked down, unwilling to see the dejection on his face.

"I can't lose you Richard. That's all. And if you go back in there you might not come out next time." She grasped his hands tightly, as if trying to force her will into his fingers. "Can't you feel how dangerous this is? Can't you feel it? The forest is evil, Richard, it always has been. You must know that now, after what it's done to you?"

He dropped her hands like they were on fire and marched to the window, annoyed that she had fallen into the same trap as the rest of the town, blaming the Blackhart instead of the madman who chose to abduct his victims there. "I thought you were smarter than that, Katrina, I really did. How can a forest be evil? It's just a place, for God's sake. Like this house, or... or the park, or the school!" He started to shout, angry that he should have to state the obvious like that, "Just because some lunatic decides to mess up some kids faces it doesn't mean the Blackhart is evil, does it? He's the one that's evil. And as for me, well, I just fell over. I was lost and tired, that's all. Jesus, I really don't see

93

what the forest has to do with any of it." It was his turn to shake his head as he stared out into the garden and to the forest's edge beyond. The light was just starting to fade and the colours shimmered prettily through the glass, showing him nothing but beauty and peace; he had no idea how anyone could see anything else so when Katrina answered him he was stunned at the cold hatred he heard in her voice.

"The Blackhart has always been evil, Richard, just look at it. It emanates blackness and fear and corruption. I wish someone would burn the whole place down." He turned to face her, clearly outraged at the prospect, "Yes, that's right, that's how much I hate it. And it has nothing to do with those poor girls, not really, they just add to it. I've always hated the place," she shuddered, "that's why I've never been in it. I'm so fucking terrified of the place I didn't even go in there to find my own sister!"

She suddenly burst into tears and Richard forgot all about being angry and went to comfort her. He finally had a vague understanding of why she was so frightened when he went into the forest, and in that moment he almost backed down and promised never to go back. But he knew that would be another lie, and he couldn't do that to her either. So he just let her cry and had the sense to stay quiet until she calmed herself.

"I'm sorry, I keep doing this. I've always been so tough, I don't know what's the matter with me these days. It's ever since you told me about Bethany, you know, I keep reliving it over and over." She paused and wiped her eyes, "I feel like I'm going nuts or something, but I can feel her in there. I know you don't believe it but I *know* it's her, I can feel it so strong, y'know? Like she's got my heart in a vice and she won't let go." She sniffed and reached for a tissue while Richard tried to avoid eye contact. She was right, he didn't believe the girl was Katrina's sister. After all, she would be twenty-nine years old by now, and the girl in the forest was ... well ... a girl. She looked around fourteen he supposed, though she could be a year or two older, but she certainly wasn't twenty-bloody-nine. So unless he was seeing a ghost, which was just as impossible because he certainly didn't believe in ghosts, then it had to be somebody else. It was a simple conclusion but he did acknowledge that it was extremely strange for her to look so very much like Bethany Rose. But surely that's all it was - a strange coincidence which Katrina could not accept because she so badly wanted her little sister to be alive. He could not think of a single thing to say which would make her feel better so he gently began to kiss her tearstained face and then her neck and then down to her breasts and her jewelled bellybutton. They made love slowly on the sofa and for that brief time the forest was forgotten as they melted together like a lingering dream, strong and safe and sublime.

It was dark when they woke up, still snuggled beside each other in a heap of clothes, and they cuddled for a while, reluctant to let go of such a sweet interlude. Richard was the first to stand up and he dressed quickly, aware of the gaping curtains and of the tiny cat sat staring at him from the chair opposite.

"I hope he wasn't watching us earlier. I don't like the idea of an audience when we're, y'know, doing stuff."

Katrina laughed loudly at his modesty. "He's just a cat you maniac! What's he gonna do, tell all the neighbours?"

"Yeah, yeah, that's not the point. I just don't like the thought of being watched OK? By anything. Besides, he's just a baby, he's too young to be seeing stuff like that."

Katrina was still laughing. "He's a cat!" She said when she caught her breath, "a small furry animal. What? You think he'll be mentally scarred for life because he saw your big lovely cock?" She teased him, a mischievous glint in her eyes, knowing all too well how embarrassed he would be at her language. He took the bait immediately.

"Katrina!" His shocked tone never failed to amuse her. It was as though he had never heard such words before, as though he was still a virgin or they were in a church or his parents were there. "You can't say things like that! Someone might hear."

She stood up, still completely naked, and walked towards him "And who exactly is going to hear me, darling?" She made a show of turning a full circle and looking round the room, aware that he was looking only at her body and deliberately moving closer so she could slowly undo the buttons on his jeans. "Or, more to the point, who's going to hear you when I take you in my mouth and make you .."

His eyes widened as the doorbell rang but Katrina just giggled and pushed his jeans down to his ankles. "Katrina! There's someone at the door!" He couldn't help but laugh himself now as she continued to seduce him, saying "so they'll have to come back later," but the bell rang again and his curiosity won over his lust. He pushed her away amiably and buttoned his jeans for the second time. "It's late, hon', I'd better see who it is, OK?" He seemed not to notice that she was still naked and rushed through into the hallway only to return, panicking, a second later.

"Get dressed, quick!" He gathered up her clothes in a bundle and thrust them into her hands, still half amused but beginning to show signs of annoyance that she still wanted to tease him. Then he saw a worried look appear through the devilment and she began to

96

dress hurriedly.

"Hold on, I'm coming." He yelled into the hallway and then looked questioningly at his dishevelled girlfriend. "What's up? What is it?" He asked, for some reason whispering. But she whispered back and then he was as worried as she was, "It's the cops. And I think they're really pissed off."

**

Bethany was pissed off too. For the first time Richard had surprised her, and she was not used to being surprised. She had known he was coming but she had expected him to arrive much later, so she was still trying to save the girl when she felt his footsteps touch the Forest floor and for a moment she was so flustered that she almost allowed her to wake up. But she recovered just in time and tried to forget about him until it was done. She could still feel him running but she knew that this was more important, that he would have to wait for once, even if it meant she didn't see him at all today. She knew he would come back but she hated to be caught off guard and she would be far too weak to deal with him after the healing. Especially as this time it had been so much harder. This girl was slightly older and she struggled constantly against the sleep, fighting all the time and trying so hard to open her eyes. Bethany had become quite impatient with her by the time she felt Richard enter her domain, so it was easy for her concentration to slip as she tried to soothe such an uncooperative patient. What she hadn't noticed though, was that the girl had actually seen her. That for a tiny fraction of a second when she had gasped in surprise the girl's eyes had flickered open and taken in the shocked expression on her face, and the way her hands sparked and trembled upon her own face, which seemed to sting and ache and burn. And although Bethany would never know it, the girl would remember that moment for the rest of her life, it would haunt her nightmares and prey upon her waking dreams when she least expected it. But for now she was paralysed again, lost in a controlled comatose state, as Bethany concentrated all her powers on the healing and left Richard to wait at the clearing, pacing and frustrated.

He waited a long time, sometimes sitting, seemingly patient and calm, other times walking up and down in agitation and venturing each time further beyond the Elm to try his luck at finding the mysterious barefooted girl who had become his obsession. Bethany tried to find her way to him, after it was finished, but the girl's mind was so hard to program that she daren't leave her like the others, and had to stay close to keep her asleep until it was dark. She took her to the fern-bed she had made next to the pathway, moving her limbs carefully with her mind, and as she lay her down for the final rest she almost collapsed alongside her, but she knew she must not give way just yet, so she hid inside a huge holly bush and tried to focus. She had done this easily before, speaking gently to the girls' minds to ensure they slept on until it was safe to wake, but for some reason this girl had closed off her mind completely, and she knew there was no other option but to hold the sleep herself and therefore end it herself, which meant she could not go and rest, and she certainly could not go to Richard. She did try though, she thought that maybe she could hold the girl's coma from a distance, but as she moved through the forest she felt her stirring and rushed to return, for she knew the scars would not be set if she woke whilst there was still light in the sky.

So Richard would not be able to see her that day, nor she him, and Bethany was greatly annoyed with herself for having timed everything so badly and she was cross with the girl for being so difficult to manage. Her anger was felt through the ground she sat on and the bush which surrounded her. It was felt in the roots of the trees and up through their trunks to the very tips of their leaves. And the creatures of the forest were angered too, they stamped and growled and fought until the Blackhart grew stormy and rebellious. It searched Bethany's heart and saw only that Richard was to blame for her disquiet and it began to circle the clearing, raging against his presence with sharp gusts of wind and tremors in the ground. Richard, who had no intention of getting caught in a storm inside the forest, was oblivious to the wrath which surrounded him and, as he ran home, equally annoyed at the girl for not being there, he attributed his sudden queasiness and apprehension to the growing squall. When he finally reached his garden gate the weather was calm once more, but he was so relieved to reach his house unscathed that it did not occur to him to wonder why, and as the forest settled behind him only Bethany remained upset. She sat cross-legged in the centre of the bush, barely conscious now, but holding tight to her anger like a crutch to keep her from collapse. And before her the girl lay sleeping, caught in a spell but fighting all the time to wake up. She would wake up, but much later, when the last of the light had left the sky and when Bethany fell into her own deep sleep, only then would she wake up, Trinity May Brown, the third victim of the Blackhart scarrings, and then she would wish that she had never woken up at all.

15

DC Hobbs

Detective Constable Hobbs had wasted no time in reporting Richard Haley to his Sergeant when he had spotted him running wildly through the forest earlier in the day. He had been convinced on their previous meeting that Mr Haley was lying about his own incident in the Blackhart and seeing him there so soon after the event only served to add to his suspicions. He had wanted to arrest him at the time but he had been too far away to catch up with him, so he had simply reported the sighting immediately and voiced his misgivings to his superior, namely Detective Sergeant Cummings, a tall and upright officer who, unfortunately for Hobbs, was not about to arrest a man for being fit and healthy. Hobbs did try to point out that the forest had been declared off limits to the general public but DS Cummings was a runner himself, and also quick to point out that they could hardly cordon off the whole of the Blackhart. As far as he was concerned, there was nothing at all to link Richard Haley to the scarrings and DC Hobbs should in future keep his baseless opinions to himself.

So Hobbs cursed his boss and continued to keep watch as was his duty. It was a warm and pleasant evening but as the sun began to set he became increasingly apprehensive, jumping even at his own shadow, and startled by every rustle in the undergrowth. This jittery state was not something Hobbs was used to. He was a big man in general, plus he had a set of weights in his garage and he worked out for an hour every day, he played rugby every Sunday and he hadn't lost a fight since he was ten - so he was not usually a man given to bouts of nervousness. Tonight, however, he felt like he was somebody else. He felt an almost tangible charge of dread in the air and the very ground he stood on seemed to squirm and chafe at his feet until he found himself moving gradually towards the exit he was supposed to be watching. He had no idea why he was suddenly so afraid and he hated to admit to himself that that was actually what he was feeling, but the trees seemed to close in on him, seemed to push him backwards while the earth rolled and the breeze whispered sullen threats in his ears. He tried to laugh at himself, to separate what was surely the tricks of his imagination from the dull reality of the forest pathway he had been standing by all afternoon, but it didn't work, and as his breathing became shorter he realised that he would not be able to stay for much longer, that his feet were moving without his permission and that, if he wasn't careful, he would be running from the forest in the same wild manner as Mr Haley, which is to say extremely fast and with very little control.

When the phone rang he actually screamed, but somehow the moment he pulled the small piece of modern technology from his pocket his fear dissolved completely and he even managed to answer with a relatively calm voice.

"Hobbs here."

"Hobbs? Cummings. You seen anything else? Only we just had a girl reported missing, never showed up at her friend's house this morning, parents out for the day, that sort of thing." He trailed off, muttering something inaudible under his breath, "Anyway Hobbs, what of it?"

"No Sir, nothing more to report, well, nothing I can explain really." He spoke the last part quietly, his voice a little shaky after his recent experience, but the Sergeant picked up on it instantly.

"What do mean Hobbs, what's happened there? Because if you're buying into all this witchcraft voodoo nonsense that's flying around I won't listen to any of it, is that clear?" Cummings liked to answer his own questions and spoke in a hurried staccato which allowed no interruptions. "So either you can explain it or it didn't happen, that's for sure. Well? Good. So? Anything more to report? This Haley chap been back?"

Hobbs relaxed and made a mental note never to mention his strange experience in the forest. He convinced himself that he had just let his imagination run riot for a few minutes and as he spoke to DS Cummings he soon forgot completely how terrified he had been just a few minutes earlier. He was happy that Haley's name had been remembered and when his boss suggested a visit to his house he was only too pleased to comply, despite the fact that his shift would be finished shortly and he had been ordered to make a thorough search of the crime scene beforehand.

The two previous victims had both been placed in the same spot after their abduction, so Hobbs immediately set off to search that area first. He knew exactly where it was but he had previously only seen it in the daytime, so as he wandered up the pathway he misjudged the layout of shrubs along the path's edge and unknowingly made a thorough inspection of entirely the wrong area. He checked both entrances to the pathway and moved as far beyond, in both directions, as he dared. But he was not as conscientious as he should have been. He firmly believed that the girl would be found at Haley's house and he was in such a hurry to be the one to find her and, of course, to be the one who took all the glory for catching the Blackhart Scarrer, that he walked right past Trinity Brown three times before concluding that his work there was finished and rushing off to meet his boss. He checked with his replacement on the way out, commiserating with him briefly for his bad luck in drawing the night shift, and as he stepped over the threshold of the Blackhart and onto the smooth tarmac of the lamp-lit street he pretended not to notice the warm flood of relief which enveloped his body and overpowered his senses. He focussed instead on Mr Richard Haley, and on Miss Trinity Brown, who was Hartsbridge's very own answer to Naomi Campbell, and he just hoped like Hell they wouldn't be too late.

**

As Richard finally went to answer the door, Katrina, now fully dressed, did her best to straighten up the living room and make both it, and herself, a little more presentable. For her own sake, she was not at all bothered if the police recognised the disarray for what it was, but she knew that Richard would be extremely embarrassed if he thought they would be able to guess the recent activities, so she hurriedly rearranged cushions and ran a brush through her hair, hoping that her flustered boyfriend would at least have the sense to keep them talking in the hallway for a few minutes so the room would be composed by the time they entered it. Of course, she needn't have worried, Richard was a true expert at turning on the famous Haley charm even in the most difficult situations, and she had more than enough time to tidy up whilst trying desperately to listen in on the conversation occurring on the other side of the wall. From what she could tell, the cops were unimpressed at being kept waiting but Richard was placating them with a half-truth of having fallen asleep on the settee and acting very shocked and just a little annoyed at being disturbed at such a late hour.

When he showed them through to the lounge he made her smile by clearing his throat quite theatrically beforehand, but when she saw the stern faces that greeted her the smile instantly disappeared and she knew at once that her first impressions had been correct: something had happened to upset them and this wasn't just going to be a friendly chat.

Richard began to make introductions but was cut off brashly by a tall, angular man who looked about forty but had the low, gruff voice of someone much older. He had a long pointed nose and piercing grey eyes which immediately took in every object in the room, flitting sharply from one corner to the next as he spoke quickly and made no apologies for the intrusion.

"This is DC Hobbs," he gestured loosely as he talked, "you've met before I believe, this is WPC Hamshere and I'm Detective Sergeant Cummings. You must be Katrina Rose, am I right? Yes. And as I've just explained we need to speak to Mr Haley quite urgently." He broke off purely to breathe before continuing and Katrina noticed for the first time how impatient DC Hobbs was becoming as he rhythmically clenched and unclenched his fists and shuffled his feet. Clearly the Sergeant had noticed this too for he glared openly at the DC as he resumed his address, "Sit down, can we? Good. Stop you fidgeting at any rate Hobbs." They all began to sit apart from Katrina who expertly pre-empted his next words and moved towards the kitchen, "Coffee would be appropriate don't you think? Very late, tired, lots to talk about. Thank you Miss Rose. Right then ..."

Katrina decided against interrupting to find out who took what in regards to milk and sugar and disappeared into the kitchen to return with a tray so they could all add their own. Richard seemed speechless at the sheer audacity of DS Cummings but at the same time he found himself liking the man and almost admiring his forward manner. Besides, he figured it would make the visit much shorter with a man like that asking all the questions, especially if he continued to answer half of them himself. But, just as he was warming to the Sergeant, he finally realised why they had brought along the WPC and the reality of being considered a suspect left him cold and understandably hostile.

Cummings had asked in his usual blunt manner if it would be possible for WPC Hamshere to have "a quick look around the house". He did explain briefly that he was under no obligation to agree to this but that his answer would "greatly reflect upon him in relation to the case", whatever that meant. Richard and Katrina shared a startled glance as they both wondered why he was under suspicion in the matter but Cummings seemed to read their minds and went on to disclose that Mr Haley had been seen by DC Hobbs running in the forest earlier that day. Hobbs still looked ready to burst and had, in fact, begun grinding his teeth horribly, despite constant angry stares from his superior. When Richard had grasped the seriousness of the situation he did not hesitate in allowing the search, and they were all relieved when Cummings told Hobbs to go with the WPC and he left the room swiftly, forging forward like a hungry tiger on his first hunt.

There was a moment's silence as the three of them watched him leave but Katrina, who hadn't yet spoken at all, determined to ask a few questions herself before the Sergeant took over again.

"I take it there's another girl missing then? That's what Hobbs is so excited about. He thinks she's here?" She spoke quietly, sad at the thought of another victim with a face like the one she had seen.

"Yes luv, 'fraid so." Cummings was more interested

in Richard's reaction and turned back to face him after answering her, "Hobbs really has got a bee in his bonnet about you Sir, no doubt about it. Won't find a thing though, will he, eh? No, not a thing, that's for sure, poor chap. Young man you see, very eager they are at that age, doesn't know a thing really, sees you running around, which was mighty foolish wouldn't you say Mr Haley? Yes, of course. Just out for a run were you, or is there something more to it I wonder? Hobbs certainly seems to think so. Says you looked like you were running away from something. Pretty fast he says, not like your average afternoon jog. What of it Haley? Anything to report, Sir?"

Richard had broken eye contact with the Sergeant about half way through his little speech and seemed to be wishing he had x-ray eyes to see straight through the curtains and out into the night. He hesitated for just long enough to convince Cummings he was lying and then proceeded to tell the truth, which was that he was running from the storm he had felt brewing in the atmosphere. As he hadn't actually seen his mysterious girl this time, or, in fact, done anything other than run and wait and run some more, he did not, actually, have anything to report at all. Cummings, however, was a keenly intelligent man and had the precision observation skills of a hawk which had been trained to see even better than it did naturally, and he was well aware that there was much more to Mr Haley's 'running' than he was letting on. Yet, for some reason, he also did not view Haley as a suspect in this case, as, unlike Hobbs, he could not imagine the man to be anything other than the good-natured, country-loving school teacher he saw before him, so he was not remotely surprised when Hobbs and Hamshere returned empty-handed and despondent.

Richard barely glanced at them as they re-entered

the room but Hobbs was not a man to give in easily and when Sergeant Cummings excused himself to visit the bathroom (obviously wanting to have a quick look around himself) the young DC began to quiz both Richard and Katrina on every aspect of their movements throughout the day. He was clearly most annoyed that Richard had ignored all protocol to enter the Blackhart in the first place and warned him quite severely against returning to the forest in the future. Katrina had looked at her boyfriend quite pointedly during this admonition and the exchange did not go unnoticed by Hobbs, who immediately asked if she had been aware of his intentions before she left. Katrina found that question extremely hard to answer. After all, Richard had not told her or hinted in any way that he may be going into the forest, yet she had known full well that he was in there. She was also greatly puzzled at Hobbs' conviction of Richard's guilt, and was shocked to find herself wondering if he had told her the full truth about his incidents in the Blackhart. Consequently she began to feel threatened by the ongoing interrogation and was openly glad when DS Cummings marched back into the room. Hobbs was silenced with an emphatic frown, and as the Sergeant stayed standing he quickly recognised it was time to leave and made his way out to the car without even saying goodbye. WPC Hamshere, who up until now had not said a single word to either of them, shook both their hands politely and apologised in a small, squeaky voice for any inconvenience. Cummings waited with apparent impatience for her to finish and seemed to shoo her out of the front door before thrusting a small card into Richard's hands.

"Whatever it is Haley, you should spit it out before it chokes you, that's my advice, Sir. Don't like to admit it you see, but we have no bloody clue what's going on with these blasted scarrings so if you know anything at all you'd do well to come forward. Yes, very well indeed. Before young Hobbs here gets carried away, you see. Young Detective Constables have so much imagination these days, Sir, and I shouldn't like to have to interview you down at the station next time." He paused for effect but there was none and the threat dissipated as he charged on in his typical clipped fashion. "So you won't want to be running around in the forest anymore will you? No. Plenty of nice parks around here Haley, aren't there? Yes, parks. Anyway, you'll call me when you decide to get it off your chest, I'm sure, yes. Goodnight Miss Rose, knew your father you know, bloody good man." And he slammed the door behind him.

16

Trinity

Trinity Brown had been allowed to wake up at around the same time that DC Hobbs had been sent to search the crime scene, and she had prayed fervently that whoever was wandering around with the torch would not see her. As both her skin and her clothes were black, it was quite easy for her to shrink into the ground and remain hidden, providing she kept her eyes and mouth shut tight so their bright white contrast was invisible. She couldn't quite believe how often he walked past her, the torch beam rolling right over her at times while she held her breath and urged him silently to keep on walking. But then when he finally left she felt alone and less relieved than she had expected, wondering why she had so desperately wanted to remain concealed in this dark and frightful place. Of course she soon remembered why, and she soon stopped being frightened. After all, the thing to be frightened of had already happened, so what did it matter.

She sat huddled on the makeshift fern-bed, quietly amazed at how comfortable and warm it was, and tried to think about what she should do. Purely by instinct she knew that her face was ruined. It didn't hurt at all, and she hadn't yet dared to touch it, but somehow it just felt wrong in itself, and she vowed there and then never to look in a mirror, for she felt she would go completely mad if her beautiful features were not there looking back at her. And she couldn't bear to go home either, her parents would probably faint or start screaming like Zoe's mum was supposed to have done, and that would be the worst thing surely, to be so hideous that your own mother screams at the sight of you. Jesus. She shuddered at the prospect and her eyes filled with tears. She was going to be a model, for God's sake. She already had a portfolio and everything. It was all so easy with her dad being a photographer and everybody constantly telling her how perfect she was, with her sharp cheekbones and her naturally pouting lips. And of course she had the perfect model figure as well: tall and skinny with hip bones like razors and breasts like a young boy. Why that was in any way attractive she had never understood but she was the envy of all her friends and they hated it when she pigged out on pizza and ice cream every night without putting on a single pound or sprouting even the tiniest of spots. Her parents, who were obsessively religious and attributed everything good to 'Our Lord' and everything bad to 'the temptations of Satan', had told her repeatedly that she had been blessed with the face of an angel so that wherever she went in the world she would bring happiness to those who saw her. Trinity thought that was total crap but she had been looking forward to earning a lot of money and wearing designer clothes, and besides, being a model was the only thing she knew how to be, it was what she had been born for and the only thing she had ever wanted.

So she pretended for a while that it was all just a bad dream. She tried to go back to sleep and imagined waking again in her own bed, happy and relieved to be free from such a strange nightmare, and looking forward to meeting Rachel for a day of glorious shopping and no school. She imagined walking up the hill and deciding to take the long way round to her friend's house after all, because they had been told not to go into the forest under any circumstances, and never mind that she would be late, Rachel wouldn't mind waiting for her and it would only take an extra twenty minutes. But Trinity didn't like walking. She had asked her folks for a lift but they had been in a rush to get to some church charity thing and didn't have time to 'hang around while you mess about in the bathroom for hours'. So she had had to walk. And she hadn't realised just how long she had spent in the bathroom - she had wanted to look her best in case she accidentally bumped into the sales guy she was crazy about in Next - until she went downstairs to get breakfast and saw the clock on the microwave. Breakfast had turned into a Mars Bar en route and suddenly the forest path, which was not only out of bounds but incredibly scary, had become extremely inviting.

Trinity tried to hold on to her dream of avoiding the Blackhart and hoped beyond hope that she really was in a nightmare, but she remembered the reality all too well and she knew that that one simple decision had been her undoing and she could not take it back, as much as she might wish to. So she forced herself to sit up and make another decision. It was pitch black in the forest now, which meant it was very late and her parents must be worried sick. It was also starting to get cold and she could probably die of shock or pneumonia or something if she stayed here all night, so she knew she should really go home. Yet home was the one place she just could not face going to. She almost smiled at the ironic use of words in her thoughts but her mouth felt tight and strange and she began to cry again. She couldn't bear for her parents to see her like this but she did want them to know she was OK, well, that she was alive at any rate. So she had to go somewhere and phone them.

Still crying, Trinity Brown finally stood up and, after rummaging on the floor to find her bag she was surprised to find that nothing had been stolen and she had plenty of change for a phone call. Not for the first time, she cursed her parents for not allowing her a mobile like the rest of her friends (and the rest of the world, she thought bitterly) and tried to think where the nearest telephone box would be that hadn't been smashed up. She knew there was one near the school but she was more likely to be seen up there, as it was very well lit and nearer to the main road, but the only other one she could think of was a lot further away and meant a long trek in the dark. She stood, undecided, as the tears flowed down her cheeks and she half-wished she had let the torch-man find her after all, at least then all the decisions would be made for her. But then she realised that for the first time in her life she was having to think for herself and she began by fishing out her tissues and bravely wiping her eyes and blowing her nose. She didn't let her hands linger on her face too much but nevertheless it was impossible not to feel the scars and she instantly started to shake as the tears rose again and she almost cried out. But she was determined to be strong, to somehow survive this without going completely insane and to keep some shred of dignity intact despite her life being in tatters. She wondered how Katherine Katson and Zoe Bishop had coped at this point. No-one was supposed to know the names of the scarring victims but it was easy to see who didn't come to school anymore and it was impossible not to hear the rumours - that Katz had to be sedated constantly and spent most of the time unconscious, and how Zoe had locked herself in her room for days, practically starving to death before she allowed anyone inside. Trinity knew they were just rumours though, and she wasn't sure what to believe. She didn't really know either of the two girls for they were both in the year below her, but everyone knew Zoe Bishop because of the crazy band she had set up. It was actually quite good, despite the punk style clothing and the angry lyrics, and Trinity remembered seeing them at a school concert one evening and thinking that Zoe must have a lot of guts to get up there like that in front of everyone. She tried to remember the name of the band but all she could think of was Zoe's cute face, and she realised for the first time that she wasn't alone after all.

She had no idea what she was going to say when she got there but Trinity Brown set off for Zoe Bishop's house at a pace which could almost be considered a slow run, which was quite impressive for someone whose idea of exercise was strutting and posing for half an hour in front of her dad's camera. She knew where it was because of all the activity that constantly surrounded both girls' houses - a seemingly endless rotation of police cars, doctors and journalists that utterly ridiculed the promise of anonymity made by each party. The newspapers could not print names but they could send photographers to camp outside the poor girl's houses just in case one of them forgot she was horrifically deformed for a moment and decided to answer the doorbell. It was sick really, but it did mean that Trinity finally knew where to go to try and find a refuge for the night. She knew that Katherine was from the posh end of town so it was easy to work out where the two girls lived, and, if her sense of direction was working properly, what was even better was that Zoe's house was fairly near the forest anyway, and if she was careful she would be able to approach it from the back, which meant that hopefully no-one would see her at all.

As Trinity emerged from the Blackhart, scratched and out of breath from her frequent stumbles in the darkness, she crouched low as she scurried across the field which separated the forest from a row of small terraced houses and their back gardens. She had worked out that Zoe's house was on the corner at the far end of the field but she wanted to be absolutely sure before she tried to get in, which meant that somehow she would need to see the front of the house as well, which could still be being watched, even at this late hour. But as she half ran, half crawled up through the open gate at the bottom of the garden she was surprised to see a soft light shining down from an upstairs window and she looked up instinctively, without thinking. She realised her mistake too late but as she did so she also realised that at least she would not need to go around to the front of the house, for the masked face staring down at her told her instantly that she had come to the right place, and she only hoped that Zoe would understand why she had come here and not just freak out or call the cops.

She had no need to worry. Over the last few days Zoe Bishop had learnt that she didn't actually want to die after all and so she had been forced to develop an inner strength which few people truly possess. She had taken to wearing many different masks, which she had persuaded her brother to buy from a fancy dress shop, and she felt more comfortable now that her family no longer looked at her with a mixed expression of pity and nausea. The masks amused her too, she liked the scary ones best, and she found it interesting that a mask of a hideous distorted face was more acceptable to others than the same reality underneath the mask. Despite her new found fortitude, though, Zoe still had problems sleeping at night, a condition which, she would have been curious to discover, also affected Katherine Katson, contrary to the opposing rumours. She was afraid to fall asleep lest she find herself back in the forest again, having lost a whole day and with no memory of anything, which was the one aspect of the whole ordeal which continued to disturb her the most, how something so dreadful could happen without even getting the chance to fight back. It left her cold and angry and generally reluctant to go to bed, so she liked to sit at night with her headphones on and write twisted lyrics which she imagined someone else would sing one day while she hid behind her masks and collected the royalties.

In spite of everything, she still had her hopes of fame and fortune and it was while she was dreaming of a grand masked ball where no-one was beautiful that she suddenly heard what sounded like footsteps in the garden and she peered through the window. It was very dark but she could clearly see a thin figure crouched and frozen on the lawn, bright white eyes staring fearfully back at her. She couldn't quite make out the features to know who it was but, as she continued to watch, the figure slowly stood up and gestured first at his or her own face and then at the window where Zoe stood. Initially she was terrified, and almost called out, but then curiosity overcame her as the gesture was repeated and she was confused for only a few small seconds. The recognition shook her when it came and she took a step back from the window in panic. She had thought at first it must be Katherine but the figure was tall and black and looked more like a boy so she looked properly again and finally understood that it had happened for a third time. Her eyes filled with tears and she felt strangely moved that this third victim had chosen to come to her for help, so she motioned for the figure to stay put and keep quiet and she hoped the frantic waving was understood as she crept downstairs and opened the back door.

There was complete silence as the two girls stared solemnly at each other for what seemed like an age. Trinity was waiting for some sort of horrified reaction to her twisted features but of course she could see no expression but the warped grin on the green witch's mask which stood before her. Under the mask, Zoe was actually smiling, a rare occurrence these days, as for the first time since her scarring she felt a real glimmer of hope beginning to surface. She had not realised until this moment just how lonely her life had become and although she was sad for someone else to suffer her fate she instantly felt the kinship they shared in their damaged state. So, as she took Trinity's hand she broke the silence and whispered two simple words which calmed her new friend's frightened eyes at once,

"It's OK."

They went up to Zoe's bedroom together and after Trinity had called her parents they decided to make just one more phone call, to their other scar-sister Katherine Katson, who told them straight away (between poignant sobs and sniffs) that it was Katz, not Katherine, "and you spell that with a 'z' not an 's', OK?"

17

DS Cummings

"That was weird."

Richard and Katrina still stood in the hallway and stared at the front door as if waiting for it to open again. Katrina had voiced both their feelings with the statement and even when they heard the police car drive away they remained in the hall, Katrina leaning against the wall with her arms crossed protectively and Richard slumping down on the stairs and cradling his cast. They looked at each other and back at the door as if not quite believing it was over and when Katrina spoke Richard finally seemed to grasp the precarious situation he had consigned himself to. He ran his fingers through his hair, obviously distressed, and Katrina came to sit beside him.

"They think it's me, don't they? I can't believe it. How could they think that?" He looked at her beseechingly and she shook her head at him, firm and emphatic.

"No baby, they don't think it's you at all, they just had to rule you out 'cause that Hobbs guy saw you in the Forest. The only other reason they're suspicious is that we're both terrible liars and it's bloody obvious to anyone with half a brain that something else is going on here." She took his hand to stop the nervous hair-touching and forced him to look at her. "But that doesn't mean they think you did anything. It just must be hard for them to know you're hiding something when this is such a horrible case. Especially if they really have got nothing to go on. I mean, God, there's been another one already and the Sergeant said they had no leads at all. I mean, that's dreadful! It's like it's gonna go on forever or something!" She trailed off, deep in thought. "Those poor, poor girls. I wonder who it was this time. Mind you, whoever it was must've been crazy to go into the forest in the first place. Do young people just not have any fears at all these days? Or any sense for that matter?" Katrina suddenly stopped as she realised that Richard was looking even more stressed than before. "What is it? What did I say?"

He stood up and grabbed his jacket from where it had been casually slung over the banister rail and she instantly understood what he meant to do. She moved quickly in front of him and would not let him pass. "No way, Richard. You're not going anywhere, I mean it."

"Why not?" He was clearly upset but he didn't try to push past her and she knew he wouldn't, he was too much of a gentleman, so he tried to explain instead. "Don't you get it? There's another girl out there about to have her face mashed up! I have to find her. I have to find her right now!" He wasn't quite shouting but it was close, and Katrina felt his frustration vividly, but she also knew that the girl he wanted to find was not the poor girl who had just been reported missing, and his obsession with her sister was starting to annoy her immensely. Well, if she was honest, it was actually starting to really scare her, which only served to fuel her irritation because she couldn't quite pinpoint why she was so scared. Not that any of that mattered at the moment. The only thing she cared about at this precise second was preventing the man she loved more than anything in the world from going to the place she hated more than anything in the world and she was quite prepared to knock him out cold with a frying pan if that was the only way to do it. Katrina almost laughed aloud as the image popped into her head and she decided to try talking to him first.

"The why doesn't really matter. You are not going into the forest tonight, full stop. And don't look at me like that!" He was glaring at her viciously. "I'm doing this 'cause I love you, can't you see that? And if that's not a good enough reason then I've loads more if you want to hear them." He said nothing so she continued, still blocking his path and becoming more forceful with every sentence. "OK fine. You're too late, for one. It's already happened. And don't ask me how I know that I just do. Partly the timing of the others and partly I can just feel it. And I don't care if you believe in all that instinct stuff or not. I know it's true so you'll just have to take my word for it, OK? And then there's the fact that we just had the bloody CID all over the house and you think you're gonna get two foot inside the Blackhart right now without getting arrested? I don't think so." He was starting to droop like a naughty schoolboy who had just realised he wasn't going to get away with it this time. "And then, of course, there's the big one. It's just too fucking dangerous! Quite apart from the fact that it's pitch black in there and you'll never find her anyway. Jesus. I thought you were meant to be the clever one in this relationship?"

Richard had already dropped the jacket on the floor and appeared so dejected yet furious at the same time that Katrina wasn't sure if he was going to scream at her or just burst into tears. Finally he just made a peculiar growling noise and hugged her until she could barely breathe. They went back into the lounge together and Katrina poured them both a large whisky 'as a night-cap' but they soon discovered that neither of them was at all sleepy so they hunted out the box with the DVD's in and settled down to watch a movie instead. They watched in silence until about half way through the film when Katrina suddenly sat up and said "Huh" for no apparent reason. Richard looked at her questioningly and she pressed pause before turning to him.

"There was no storm today." She said, clearly confused.

"What?" Richard was as confused as she was.

"There was no storm. You said you were running out of the forest because you felt a storm brewing. But there wasn't a storm, was there?"

He quickly grasped her line of thought and shrugged, vaguely recalling the wind and the pressure of a building storm but realising for the first time that the weather had indeed been fine when he got home. "No, I guess there wasn't," he answered, "but I definitely felt something in there. The winds picked up and everything felt kind of, oh, what's that word . . ." he clicked his fingers and searched his vocabulary impatiently, ". . heavy, no, oppressive. That's the one, oppressive," he seemed satisfied to have found the correct word and looked back at her impassively, "I guess it must have blown over or something."

"Yeah, I guess so." Katrina tried to keep the scepticism from her voice as he took the film off pause and settled down again. She watched the rest of the movie in a daze and snuggled close to her boyfriend, loving how safe she felt just curled up against the muscles of his chest and arms. But no matter how safe she felt being close to him, she still couldn't shake off her fear of the forest, and for every warm thought of affection and security she enjoyed, she suffered an opposingly cold vision of darkness and torment, where the very trees themselves sneered and roared as the Blackhart rose up to destroy them both. And in the midst of all this misery and mayhem Bethany stood alone, crying and bewildered as the world caved in around her, screaming out in horror for her sister to save her as she sank into the soil and slowly disappeared. Katrina had seen this vision in her nightmares but it seemed worse to her to be awake and to have no control over the images in her head. So she clung tightly to Richard and waited for it to pass, refusing to cry until he was asleep in bed and she no longer had to try and pretend to be strong. Then she cried. She cried until her head ached and her eyes were swollen and her nose was sore and blocked and her cheeks were stinging from wiping the tears over and over. She cried until she slept, exhausted, and she was still asleep when Richard came downstairs in the morning and wrote her a note explaining that he had to go into the forest to find the girl and he was really sorry but he had his mobile and he would be back by lunchtime and she mustn't worry about him. She threw up on his sofa when she read it, and after she cleaned up the mess she picked up the phone. She had meant to call Richard, but somehow she found herself staring at a small business card laying on the table, and she phoned Detective Sergeant Cummings instead.

**

Robert Cummings was already having a bad day. For a number of years now he had considered himself far too old to be in bed any later than eleven p.m. and, as he had not even arrived home the previous night until two a.m., he was extremely tired and, therefore, extremely grumpy. The argument he had had with DC Hobbs as they drove away from Mr Haley's house had been heated to say the least, and the extent of the younger man's ire still stuck in his mind. He was worried that Hobbs may be becoming a little unstable and he found this rather puzzling, considering the man's exemplary record and normally easygoing nature. But, he was not the type of person who felt capable of raising the issue and so he was very glad that Hobbs was not working today. Hopefully, the day off would cool his temper and clear his mind so that when he returned in the morning he would be back to his calm, rational self again.

Cummings wished that he had taken the day off today too. On their return to the station last night they had received a semi-hysterical phone call from Mr and Mrs Brown informing them that Trinity was at Zoe Bishop's house and had refused to come home. Seemingly, they had assumed that the police would be able to go to the house and drag their daughter out kicking and screaming, and they were not impressed when he had suggested they simply respect her wishes for the night considering the ordeal she had been through. Clearly though, it was not enough for the Browns to know that Trinity was safe, so they had driven over to the Bishop's themselves and were creating a minor riot outside the house, with the press enjoying every minute of their frenzied assault. When Cummings had arrived, still with Hobbs and Hamshere in tow, he had been amazed to see the three victims of the Blackhart scarrings standing hand in hand in the doorway, each wearing bizarre masks and showing a bravery he found both extraordinary and touching, issuing a statement to the multitude of media and refusing to be separated from each other. He had had to call in five PC's for back-up before he could clear the crowds away and after that he had suffered the more difficult job of interviewing Miss Brown, who, despite her show of courage, was obviously still in shock and fighting back sobs at every moment.

Her story was basically the same as the first two, but there was one strange addition which he had first dismissed as a dream but which bothered him more and more as he remembered the girl's conviction as she described it. She had been so sure of what she had seen that he wondered if the attacker could actually have a female accomplice, and that his original idea of a hallucinogenic drug was as impossible as the blood tests suggested. And that was another thing that riled him: all three girls had been unconscious for between twelve and twenty hours yet the medical reports shown no sign of any unusual chemicals in their bloodstream. Their adrenaline levels weren't even increased for God's sake, and other than one split second of intense burning which Miss Brown vaguely recalls, none of them recounted feeling any sort of pain or discomfort or *anything* either during or after the event. It had been suggested that the perpetrator was some sort of master hypnotist, and could render his victims helpless purely through mind control, but Cummings was ever the sceptic and besides he had questioned various experts on the subject and even they had said that it could not possibly be done that way. So, he was left with nothing, again, except maybe the face of a girl who, according to Trinity, was younger than her and had hands which glowed and flickered like electricity.

It had bothered him all day, such a precise and confident description which also seemed a fantastical nonsense and, as the night's various events replayed in his mind, he became increasingly agitated at the tedious array of reports awaiting completion on his desk and the constant interruptions of harrassed-looking DC's who wanted to advise him that yet another enraged parent had called in to complain about how useless they all were.

It was just about the last straw, then, when his mobile rang and a terrified woman on the other end told him "he's gone into the forest again you see and I really don't know what to do." His first thought was

123

that they had finally found the bastard but then the voice recognition in his head kicked in and he realised that the frightened woman was Katrina Rose and the 'he' she was so worried about was none other than Mr. sodding Haley. DS Cummings sighed and told Miss Rose he'd send a couple of men to look for him but she seemed as incensed as Hobbs and he wondered briefly if madness was catching. She spoke in circles about the Blackhart being evil and something about her sister needing to be saved and before he knew what he was saying he had promised to go round there himself and "sort everything out". Not that he knew what there was to sort out, but what he did know was that Katrina Rose had a story to tell about her boyfriend and the forest, and if a story was what it took for him to finally get a handle on this God-awful case then he would be only too happy to hear it.

18

Forest & Hospital

Richard was completely lost. He did not know that Katrina was about to tell Sergeant Cummings every last detail about his experiences in the Blackhart, but what he did know was that he had been in the forest for around three and a half hours now and all he had found was more forest. He had ignored his inbuilt childhood warnings about veering off the pathways and after waiting around thirty minutes at the usual clearing he had run on past the elm and forged deeper into the woodland beyond. Now and then he thought he recognised certain areas from the first time he had chased her, but he could never be sure, and from the corner of his eye he caught constant glimpses of fur and eyes belonging to creatures he could not quite see but he was sure were following him again. He tried to stay calm and run steadily, taking in his surroundings and mapping out a route to take him back, but after a while he was too tired to run and too tired to think, and instead he just wandered aimlessly, shouting out the occasional 'hello?', the noise of which seemed to dissipate silently into the trees rather than booming loudly through them as he had expected. He had been trying to find the stream he remembered so clearly from that first mystical encounter but it eluded him as completely as did the girl herself, and after a while he began to wonder what the Hell he was doing here at all.

By the time his girlfriend picked up the phone that day, Richard Haley was deep in the Blackhart, lost again, and feeling more than a little annoyed at his continuing misfortune. His exasperation was fuelled by the fact that all the hairs on his arms had been stood on end for about the past hour now, and by the intense prickling sensation on the nape of his neck which seemed to increase with every step, both of which told him that he was not alone here and that he should have listened to his girlfriend's warnings. But, on occasion, he could be as stubborn as she was and this appeared to be one of those occasions. For some reason he was committed to this obsession and a modicum of fear was not about to stop him. Besides, he was lost anyway, so he couldn't just turn around and head for home even if he wanted to. And there was a part of him that did want to do exactly that; to turn and flee and scream as if the hounds of Hell had been set upon him and were gnashing at his heels. But there was yet another part of him, a much bigger part, which compelled him to keep searching, to keep moving and calling out until she appeared from behind the nearest tree trunk one more time, soft and shining as she always was, like a beacon of beauty before him.

But there were too many trees to look behind, and as Richard grew more and more despondent at his lack of success, so the forest became more and more irritated by his presence there. He had wandered, wholly by accident of course, very near to the Father Tree, and to the den where Bethany now lay sleeping, still exhausted from her efforts of the previous day. She had woken briefly at dawn, shocked to discover that she had allowed herself to fall asleep inside the holly bush where she had hidden, so close to the pathway and, as such, so close to detection. She had hurried back to her den instantly, tears rolling down her face as the agony in her hands overcame her when she moved, and there she had sunk into her bed thankfully, Chaver appearing from nowhere at her side, licking her swollen fingers and settling down to watch over her once again. Now that she was safe she was unlikely to wake for some time and, as her powers were so diminished by her recent work, she did not feel Richard's proximity in the slightest, despite the low growling of her friend the fox as he neared the entrance to her den. The Blackhart felt him though, for it had no need for sleep, and though he could not possibly see the den for what it was the forest was outraged that he should walk so close to her without permission, and so it began to stir. Gradually at first, with an almost deliberate stealth so as not to alarm him, and then faster and faster until the air visibly crackled with the force of it's fury. It incited the earth and rose up through the sap of the trees and the shrubs and the flowers. It coursed painfully through the blood of all the creatures who lived within its boundaries; insects, birds and animals alike began to buzz and shriek and stamp, incensed beyond measure and with no conception of the strength which moved within them. They had long since been resigned to the power of the forest and they knew no other life than that which it gave them; safe within it's boundaries they dwelt in submission to it's will and they knew it's calling could not be questioned or ignored. So they moved as one, upon a greater instinct than their own, and let their master guide them to it's bidding until it chose to free them and release the tight grip with which it pulled them closer to their prey. And as they moved they quickly lost all knowledge of their individuality. They became a single, overwhelming entity: the plants, the creatures and the earth and air they shared became a great and terrifying force which at that time had only one agenda - to destroy the intruder; the one who would hurt it's precious healer must be made to suffer.

Without Bethany to protect him Richard was soon aware that this time there would be no reprise from the wrath of the animals which had begun to gather around him. He had started to run when he had first felt the change in the atmosphere, when he had first seen and not believed that the branches of the trees were bending and twisting to scratch his face and the bracken was swerving to block his path and whip his legs at every turn. The grasses and the ground ivy seemed to swirl and wrap around his feet as if to trip him and the sweet scent of violets and foxgloves invaded his nostrils with such animosity that he felt their sickly odour would cause him to vomit or even faint as he tried in vain to get free of the plant life which impossibly seemed poised to overpower him. His mind was attempting to deny the accuracy of what his eyes were showing it, and he wondered if some mad terrorist had poisoned a batch of Nescafe with LSD to try and scare people to death. If so, he decided it was working, for his legs were becoming so entangled he could barely walk now and the low humming sound he had heard in the distance was developing into a frighteningly loud buzz which sounded like it would be upon him at any moment. He had never been scared of bees or wasps before, but then he had never heard what sounded like millions of them advancing on him with the precision of a well-trained army. He knew he had to get out of here before they arrived but each step was a struggle and he knew that if he fell down it would all be over. Adrenaline forged through his veins, his heart pounded and his brain finally admitted that the forest was trying to kill him. He fumbled for his mobile instinctively but then realised he had no clue whatsoever as to where he was so he left the tiny telephone in his back pack and reached instead for the Swiss army knife which had been there for years and had never been used. He had no escape but to fight back and he hacked away at the undergrowth with a fury born of sheer incomprehension and the offence of such an impossible attack. As he cut and slashed his way through reaching shrubs and winding roots he was amazed to watch them recoil at the touch of the blade but he had no time to stare for they quickly returned their onslaught, angry at the audacity of his retaliation. It was hard work, but with each slice of his knife the path became clearer and Richard's hopes were raised. He thought if he could just find his way back to the clearing he would be OK - after all, there was only so much mere plants could do to try and stop him from running. But no matter how far he moved, the buzzing followed him, and when he dared to glance over his shoulder he wished hadn't, for the air was so thick with insects he could not see beyond them, there was just a thick black wall of that terrible sound from floor to treetop. He panicked then, and almost tripped as a large tree root bent up towards his knees and hammered his shins harshly, yet somehow he managed to recover, his fear of falling spurring him on until suddenly the air was filled with flapping and screeching and sharp, raking claws which told him it was over.

The birds were just the beginning.

**

When Katrina stepped into the forest for the first time in her life she fully expected to drop down dead there and then. Her terror of the Blackhart had increased dramatically during the course of the day and she would not have been at all surprised to have suffered a fatal heart attack purely from the shock of what she was doing. But nothing happened. She stood there, on a narrow, well worn pathway between two bouncing bluebell rivers and waited for the sky to fall upon her, or for the ground to open up and eat her alive, or for anything similarly horrific to occur; but nothing happened. Well, that wasn't strictly true. The one major thing which happened was that she stopped shaking and she stopped crying. In fact, she stopped being scared at all. A strange calm had settled upon her that was as extreme as her previous fear and she thought the shocked expression on Sergeant Cummings' face was directed at her sudden change in behaviour. Then she noticed what had really amazed him and was amazed herself: the forest was completely silent. It was as though every living thing was holding its breath. There was no breeze, no rustling of leaves, no whisper of insect wings, no twittering or bird song of any kind. All was still and silent and yet not at all eerie. It should have been eerie, it should have been extremely unpleasant and spooky and awful. But, bizarrely, it just felt peaceful and safe, the exact opposite of everything she had foreseen and for a moment she wondered what on earth she had been so worried about. Surely no harm could come to Richard in this tranquil environment? So she tried to centre on him again and somehow, maybe because she was actually in the forest as well, she could focus on him properly for once, and then she knew she had been right to worry. She felt his injuries instantly and saw nothing but blood where his body should be and she began to run, barely aware of Cummings shouting after her and knowing only that she had to find him quickly, that it was almost too late.

The Sergeant caught up with her easily but she didn't stop so he fell into a slow jog alongside her and marvelled at how someone so incredibly slender could be so incredibly unfit. Katrina was running as fast as she possibly could and was breathing like a woman in labour and, at that moment, she was just as annoyed at her own lack of fitness, especially when she finally noticed that Cummings was with her and hadn't even broken a sweat.

"We going anywhere in particular Miss Rose? Or

have you decided to take up running as a hobby? I don't think so, no. So we are going to Richard then." He spoke as usual without a pause and Katrina wasn't sure if he expected her to answer or not. She was far too breathless to talk so she just tried a nod in his direction and he seemed satisfied. He looked extremely puzzled though and she knew he would be wondering how she could possibly know where she was going when she had explained to him back at the house that she had never been in the Blackhart before, that she had never even taken the short-cut to school like all her friends, that she was so frightened of the forest she wasn't sure if she would be able to set foot in it without fainting. Yet here she was, nowhere near the path anymore and zigzagging through the trees like a true expert, as if she had been raised here by wild animals and knew the place inside-out. In reality she had no idea how she knew where to go, she was just following her instincts, letting them guide her to the man she loved who lay dying in a small ditch between a tall silver birch and a prickly hawthorn. She almost tripped over him before she saw him, his body was so covered in leaves and twigs and feathers and fur that it was totally unrecognisable as a living person, especially with the amount of blood that surrounded him. Cummings was immediately nauseous but Katrina just knelt beside her boyfriend and kissed his swollen lips, holding his hand and speaking softly between heaving breaths as the Sergeant radioed for an ambulance. He wasn't at all sure how they were going to get Mr Haley to the ambulance, or even if they would be able to find their way back to the path again but as he was trying to figure everything out DC Hobbs suddenly burst out in front of him and the situation seemed to solve itself. Hobbs clearly was desperate to explain himself but Cummings was in no mood for long-winded excuses so he cut the man short before he could begin.

"I take it you know the way out Hobbs? Yes, of course, so lets get this man out of here shall we? Quick smart, Constable, you can tell me later what the devil it is you're doing here."

Hobbs just muttered a short "Yessir" and between them they carried Richard out of the forest, Katrina never letting go of his hand until the medics took over at the entrance. She travelled with him in the ambulance for a second time and refused to leave his side in the hospital, where the nurses cleaned and the doctors stitched and they all gave each other baffled looks as they examined the strange variety of wounds he had sustained. His right arm seemed to have the deepest scratches, with his face and head a close second, being covered in different sized puncture wounds and smaller cuts. The cast had saved his left arm but it did have teeth marks in it, as though something had been desperately trying to rip it off but had given up when it realised there was more tender flesh elsewhere. The worst wound was a deep tear at the top of his thigh, dangerously close to his groin and needing a skin graft to repair it. Only then was Katrina forced to leave him in the care of strangers and she waited, pale and sombre, holding him in her mind as they repaired the damage. She had not known what to answer when they had asked her what had happened but she had seen the looks of incomprehension on their faces and she knew they would never understand. The peculiar green friction burns on his ankles and calves had been the most unusual, with hundreds of tiny splinters embedded in the marks, but the thorns had been scary too, covering his legs from top to bottom and so deep under the skin it was as if they'd been shot from a specially made 'thorn-gun'.

It was a long time before Richard looked human

again. His clothes were in tatters so they dressed him in a hospital gown and in bandages. His bruises provided much needed colour to offset the vast whiteness in which he was attired but to Katrina he still looked like a ghost and she could barely believe it was her beautiful lover who lay there in the bed beside her. They let her sleep in the chair next to his bed but she didn't sleep very much. She sat and wondered what the Blackhart had done to him and what it had done to her sister, and as she wondered she searched for Bethany in her mind but found only sorrow and weariness. Her dreadful recurrent nightmare returned when she did sleep, so she was glad of her insomnia and tried to focus only on Richard and on the noise of the ward around her. Incredibly, he smiled when he woke up, and when he reached for her hand she grasped it so tight it was as though their fingers had fused together momentarily. In that instant she knew he would be OK and though she could not help but smile back at him, she also could not speak. They stayed like that for some time.

**

Whilst the doctors and nurses tried their best to heal Richard's wounds Bethany lay curled in the roots of the Father Tree and wept. She had been jolted awake by her sister's first step into the forest but her attention had then been torn as she realised that Richard had been brutally attacked close by. Still exhausted she had nevertheless crawled from her den intending to put an end to the assault, only to realise that the Blackhart had ceased it's efforts already, that all was quiet and subdued. She made her way slowly to the stream and drank her fill of the fresh water, wondering all the time at the hushed atmosphere which was not of her making. Her head throbbed but before she returned to her bed she needed to be sure that Richard was not badly hurt, that he would be well enough to return to her when she wanted him. She felt his pain and went to him instantly, shocked then to find him in such a lacerated state, and angry that the Blackhart would do such a thing without her permission. She had recovered just enough energy to staunch the bleeding and she made sure he would not die before she rushed away, watching, well-hidden, as her sister pounded through the trees and nearly fell upon him, frantic and horrified as she tried in vain to rouse him. Bethany had held her breath in awe at the sight of Katrina. She looked so much older, so different yet exactly the same, with those wild green eyes which matched her own and those long dark locks, tinged with a deep fiery red which no bottle could recreate. She stared, mesmerised, wishing she could call out or run to her but unable to do either for the terror which invaded her at the sight of first one big man and then another, leaving her quaking and crying silently into her hands. She felt them leave and still she cried, confounded by a complex combination of emotions which overwhelmed her senses and left her sad and bewildered. She moved through the trees restlessly and finally settled at the foot of the Father Tree, trying to understand what had happened and learning through the ebb and flow of it's viscous sap that the forest had sought only to protect her, that in the end it was because of her that Richard had been so badly maimed. And she also discovered that it was Katrina who had quelled the attack, the unmistakable force of one who shared her blood had soothed the Blackhart's rage and left it utterly speechless in wonderment, awed by another power as deep as it's own and softened by a soul so entwined with the soul of it's healer. Katrina's presence had saved Richard's life and the power of her sister's love for him left Bethany breathless and confused. Maybe she was mistaken. Maybe it wasn't Richard Dean Haley at all. Maybe it was somebody else. But the more she tried to picture another face, another voice, she more she knew that there was no mistake. It was Richard. It had always been Richard, and if her sister was in love with him then they would both have to deal with it.

So Bethany cried for herself and she cried for Katrina. She cried for Katherine and Zoe and Trinity, and for all the pretty girls who had no idea of the pain their prettiness could bring them. And finally, unbelievably, she cried for Richard too.

19

Waiting

Exactly one week later Richard was recuperating at home and becoming exceedingly frustrated. He had been discharged from the hospital and, on the same day, as if they were just waiting to hear that he was well enough, he had been summoned to the school for a 'friendly chat' with his boss, the Head Teacher of Greenhart Comprehensive, Mr Graham Tinsley. Mr Tinsley had proceeded to explain that the Parent Teachers Association had recently called an emergency meeting and had decided between them that it would be 'appropriate' for Mr Haley to take an unscheduled leave of absence for as long as was deemed necessary until he was fully recovered and until the 'current situation' had been resolved. In other words, he was being unofficially suspended because half the town were now convinced he either *was* the Blackhart Scarrer or, if not, he was certainly crazy as a coot and should not be allowed anywhere near their precious offspring.

Richard had been upset, of course, but not really surprised. Katrina had told him what to expect from the neighbours on his return and even the nurses in the hospital, whilst taking care to be unquestionably professional, had treated him coldly and kept a very wide berth. In fact, the only person, other than his suddenly doting girlfriend, who was in any way nice to him was DS Cummings, who had visited more than was strictly necessary and had even managed to make him laugh despite the pain that such facial activity caused to his many cuts and bruises. Strangely, the Sergeant seemed to believe his story of the barefooted girl which Katrina had related to him and was interested in hearing the tales first hand, requesting all the details he could remember about the clearing where he had seen her and all the places she had led him through, and to. Cummings had his men scouring the forest with a full description of the girl and, after his initial fear at being thought insane, Richard was actually glad that Katrina had poured her heart out to the man, not least because that had led them both to come looking for him, but also because he had someone else to talk to, someone who did not believe in ghosts nor that the Blackhart was trying to destroy them all. He talked freely to the Sergeant now, blaming his overactive imagination for the more bizarre elements in each incident and happy to have the understanding of a man who lived purely by logic and rational thinking. Obviously, he couldn't fully explain this latest incident, but the Sergeant seemed satisfied with his story of being attacked by some sort of wild animal and having very little memory of what type of animal, or of anything other than the initial blow followed by sketchy impressions of being clawed at as he swam in and out of consciousness before he was found. The general consensus, therefore, was that he was merely the unfortunate victim of a wild boar or a particularly aggressive fox, possibly protecting their young which he may have inadvertently stumbled across. The various smaller wounds, it had been determined, were sustained afterwards, when other creatures may have thought he was dead and were simply looking for a free meal. This chain of events was certainly much more reasonable than the real thing, and Richard was only too pleased to be given the option of agreeing to it. At night, however, his dreams knew differently and after the first two days he had been transferred to a private room so that his screams could no longer disturb the other patients.

Katrina also knew differently and she seemed to be with him all the time, a subtle reminder of the unwelcome truth. It had been nice at first, a friendly face to smile at, a hand to hold when everything ached and stung and burned before the painkillers kicked in. But, after a while, she had driven him mad. Her constant overprotective care was not something he was used to and having so much time to think finally made him realise how much she had changed since he had moved here. She had moved in with him full-time for a start, without so much as a discussion, and while he remembered being pleased that she was staying at the house so much he now wondered why he hadn't thought how odd that was, and how unusual that she never went back to her own house anymore, that she never went 'out' for the evening and then turned up three days later - which was one of her classics. It was strange to him that Katrina being there for him (for once) should actually annoy him so much, especially since he was the one who had been so eager for them to settle down and be a 'proper couple'. But the problem was that she seemed to have become obsessed with looking after him, and her endless fussing and worrying was becoming alarmingly tedious, not to mention her incessant ravings about the 'evil' Blackhart and how lucky he was to be alive. And he hated that the most because a huge part of him nagged that it was true, that the forest had tried to kill him, that Katrina had been right all along with her magic and her 'instincts' and her "there are more things under heaven and earth than are dreamt of in your philosophy" or whatever that Hamlet quote was she kept repeating. It annoyed him that she could quote things like that too, things that he was supposed to be clever at, not her. Besides, he had never really liked Hamlet, all that whinging and procrastination and not nearly enough action, well, not until the end when it all went wrong anyway, so what was the point. He realised that this was not a great attitude for a teacher of Literature but he was not too enamoured with his career choice either at the moment so he felt he had the right to enjoy these moments of bitterness. To enjoy anything he could, in fact, while he sat, bored and uncomfortable, trying to read or watch dull and ceaseless daytime television while his leg mended and his stitches simultaneously smarted and itched with increasing irritation. In short, Richard was not happy. He was bored and frustrated by day and by night he was a shivering wreck who couldn't sleep for five minutes without screaming the house down and trying desperately to kill the branches and the bees and the birds which terrorised all his dreams. He had not even told Katrina about the tree roots and the ground ivy and the hawthorn, or anything plant-related for that matter, and though they had done the least damage to him physically, he feared for his sanity every time he allowed himself to remember the reality, to remember the sheer offence he had felt at their impossible animation. He wondered what the rational Sergeant Cummings would think if he told him the truth about those things and he knew there would be a highly qualified shrink on his doorstep before he could say 'hallucination'. Because obviously that's what it was. Obviously. Brought on by fear and exhaustion, probably, and by reading too many Stephen King novels as a teenager. So he must have imagined it all, just like he must be imagining those burn marks around his ankles right now and the multitude of tiny scabs covering his body which clearly hadn't been caused by a crazed hawthorn bush spitting it's thorns at him like an AK47 on a battlefield. Luckily, however, Richard's body was recovering perfectly and very quickly, thanks to a slight residue of Bethany's healing touch which she had accidentally imprinted upon him in her panic to save him, so before long there were less and less reminders of his ordeal for him to look at. And then it was much easier to convince himself that none of it had really happened, that the lie was the reality and the rest was just a warped creation of his nightmares, designed to keep him scared, to keep him from returning to the forest, to keep him from finding the girl. Which, of course, was of the utmost importance. The police had been wholly unsuccessful in their attempts and somehow he had expected nothing else. He knew deep down that they would never find her, that they *mustn't* find her, but that she would appear to him again when she was ready and it was essential that he be well enough to go to her. Richard did not question how he knew these things, in truth, he barely acknowledged that he did know them, but he did recognise that the need to find the girl still burned in his heart and in his mind, and he knew that when his leg was fully healed he would return to the forest once more, and this time he would not leave until he saw her, until she spoke to him with that crystalline voice and he could be free again, simply to run and breathe and not to seek.

The waiting was almost unbearable, but he waited.

**

The Forest was waiting too, waiting for all the trampling and hacking to be over, and it was becoming impatient. There seemed to be a countless amount of men constantly searching and shouting and generally creating a great deal of annoyance to the balance of life it so carefully strove to maintain, and it wasn't long before various bizarre accidents began to occur. Branches fell from trees without reason, often causing serious injury to anyone walking beneath, and the ground became gradually more uneven, sometimes disappearing altogether into deep and treacherous ditches which could not be seen until it was too late. Bethany tried to help them as much as possible but the forest did not want to listen to her pleas for patience, it was not accustomed to so much chaos within its boundaries and had a limited capacity to understand human reason, so she was forced to endure it's spiteful tricks until the number of men depleted and it was able to cope once more with a smaller, less threatening amount of homosapien traffic.

By that stage, however, the policemen still assigned to search the Blackhart were extremely nervous. The scarrings had affected the whole town but, as they were the only ones allowed inside and around the crime-scene, only they knew how peculiar the forest really was. Most of them had lived in the surrounding towns and villages all their lives, and had visited the Blackhart on many occasions, using the school path as a shortcut, walking the dog or simply strolling with the family on a sunny Sunday. But the place they were so used to seemed different now. They could not explain it, most didn't even try for fear of sounding ridiculous, but they knew when they looked at each other that they all felt the same way. The accidents suffered by some of their colleagues had been extraordinary to say the least and most of them complained of feeling strangely seasick all the time, as though the very ground they walked upon was undulating slightly, trying to throw them off balance at every turn. Men who had never called in sick their whole lives began to call in sick day after day, and those that braved the job stayed in groups, tense and watchful, talking little, as though expecting the enemy to burst through the bushes at any moment. By the time they gratefully received the order to call off the search there were only five men left out of the fifty who had first been sanctioned for the job, and for the last few days they had worked so closely together they could now move as one, not needing to speak and bound by a bold sense of duty which reflected in each other's eyes and kept them from screaming. When it was over they could not understand why they weren't more relieved, but the fact that fourteen days of ceaseless searching in the darkest of atmospheres had produced nothing whatsoever may have had something to do with it. The Blackhart Scarrer was still at large, and the girl they had been told to hunt for was nowhere to be found, and with not a shred of concrete evidence to lead them to either, the weary Constables had become utterly disillusioned. Their Chief Inspector was angry and confused and the Sergeant they all respected seemed distant and lost. And then there was the rest of the town. The people of Hartsbridge who shunned them for their failure to protect their daughters, the victims' shattered parents who pleaded and yelled for a chance of revenge, and of course the poor girls themselves, who hid inside their masks and wanted to know "Why? Why me? Why this?" It was a hard time to be a cop.

**

Bethany was pleased to see them leave as well. They had slashed their way through much of her home and, in annoying the Blackhart, they had caused damage to tender spring shoots and the recently made nests of expectant mothers. Some of the mice and rabbits had even lost their offspring due to the dangerous ditches it had created and a few of the smaller birds had had their eggs destroyed as their carefully chosen trees had been dismembered. Although the men had scared Bethany she had sensed that they were much more terrified than she was, and she also knew that her fear of them, though genuine, was misplaced and unnecessary, whereas their fear was extremely well-founded. The Blackhart had toyed with them but that was all, and she had willed them to realise that they had no business here, to realise that they were wasting their time and would only end up getting hurt if they stayed much longer. She had no way of knowing if they had felt her silent messages but she was very happy when the forest began to settle again and the men returned to the edges where they would be much safer. She was also pleased that they had never managed to penetrate the centre of the Blackhart where she spent most of her days, and she wondered at the miracle of this when they had come so close yet had passed by without even a glance. She felt perhaps that the forest had protected this area so that it could not be seen, and she hoped this was the case, for it meant that she was truly secure here, and she needed that security more than anything right now.

She sat cross-legged by the stream cradling an injured dormouse in the palm of her hand. She had lost all but one of her litter to the recent events and sustained a deep gash in her side which had left her unable to nurse her remaining baby. Bethany had tried to find a surrogate mother for the infant but the other dormice were too scared to leave their nests even for her, so she had no other option but to try and heal the tiny mum as fast as possible in order to save her even tinier child. It was delicate work to mend such a deep wound on something so small, especially as she had to take extra care not to dry the precious milk, and Bethany was exhilarated when she was finally finished. She carried the mended dormouse through to her den where the baby was sleeping and watched them nuzzle together instantly, a happy reunion as the infant followed it's instincts and began to suckle. They would stay with her for a while, she knew, for they were still weak and would need her protection, but as always she was glad of the company and would ensure their safety for as long as they needed her. Chaver may drop by to see her but he had long since been taught the rules and would allow no harm to touch an animal which carried her scent, his respect for her was too great, and in return she trusted him implicitly, knowing he would protect the smaller creatures with his life to keep this rule. So she left them there, this miniature family of two, and went wandering in her newly reclaimed land to assess the damage and begin the repairs. It was almost like the old days, the days before Richard, and she relished the feelings of worth and belonging which encompassed her as she roamed, sensing that the peace and contentment which hovered on the edge of her misery were desperate to find a home within her once again. But the room they had lived in had been torn down and they could no longer be contained, so she simply enjoyed the walking and the beauty of nature and the power to heal with which she had been blessed so many years ago. The only problem was that she had not been given the power to heal herself, she needed Richard for that, and the time was nearly upon them. The Blackhart needed healing first, as did Richard's body, but it would not be long before they were both back to full health once more and then she would summon him into the forest and show him everything.

But first there was the scarrings to think about. The healings had gone very well except for the last one but that last one really had been difficult. The depths of concentration had been staggering and her ensuing weakness had nearly caused her to be discovered, and it was that which frightened her the most. For if she was ever caught they would surely take her from her home, out of the forest which she loved and which gave her life. She knew she could not survive beyond its borders and she could not risk everything with such a mistake again. So she would have to decide what to do about the scarrings, and she would have to decide quickly, for there were so many pretty girls out there and she did not have time to save them all.

20

Gemma

Katrina awoke to the sound of the doorbell and squinted at the clock. It was quarter to eight in the morning and as she could not understand why anyone would be out of bed so early she wrapped a pillow around her head and went back to sleep. Richard was already downstairs, of course, and all she heard was the opening and closing of the door before she fell back into her dream, hoping it was nobody important or that Richard would say she wasn't home if they wanted to see her. It was only a fleeting moment of worry but it was still unnecessary as the doorbell ringer was there purely to see Mr. Haley, which was the only name his early visitor knew him by.

Her name was Gemma Cooke and she was a first year pupil of Greenhart Comprehensive. Mr Haley was her new form teacher and, like all her friends, she had heard the rumours about him and not wanted to believe them. She had very much liked her new teacher and could not understand how everyone could turn against him so quickly, especially as he hadn't been arrested or anything and he hadn't been sent to a mental institution where all the mad people were. So, if he hadn't done anything wrong and he wasn't insane why was he not allowed to be her teacher anymore? She had asked her parents but they had told her not to ask stupid questions so then she had asked Mr Peel, her maths teacher, but he had just told her not to worry about it, that it was something for the 'grown-ups' to sort out. Gemma hated them all. She was sick of being treated like a child all the time, with nothing ever being explained properly and being sent to her room every time the News came on the telly. As far as she was concerned eleven year olds should not be banned from watching the News, and if they were it should at least only be on at midnight or something, when she would be asleep, which still wouldn't be fair but at least she wouldn't notice it so much. Gemma had tried to get information from everyone, she had even phoned up the Gazette and pretended to be a journalist from another paper but she had not been able to convince them that she was old enough, even with the adult voice she had been practicing for hours. So in the end she had thought, 'well, I'll just go and see him then, he seems like a nice enough man and I wasn't scared of him at school so why should I suddenly be scared of him now?' The problem was, however, that she was scared. She couldn't help it, she was just a kid after all, and apparently at a "very impressionable age", so of course she was scared because even the grown-ups were scared and that sort of thing just rubbed off on you. So she hadn't gone to see him, she had left it for a while to see what would happen, if he would come back. But the longer she left it the more frustrated she became, and the less people talked about it, and the less scary it seemed, just to drop by on her way to school and say "Hi, what's hap'nin? So are you the Blackhart Scarrer or have you just gone mad or what?" It sounded ridiculous to her now, especially as more and more people were starting to believe the myth - that it was a spirit who lived in the forest and needed the faces of pretty young girls to become human again. It was all rubbish to Gemma, she wasn't superstitious and she certainly didn't believe in evil spirits stealing faces. Such trash! And knowing that half the adults bought into that rubbish didn't give them much credibility for anything else they told her, so she finally decided it was time to be brave and see for herself if the handsome Mr. Haley (with his incredibly cute smile) really was a monster or if he was just her lovely form teacher. She knew which one her money was on and when she set off early for school that morning her parents barely noticed. She was a studious girl who hated to be late and if they thought anything at all it was just that they were lucky to have such a sensible daughter who set off in plenty of time now that the forest short-cut could not be used.

When Richard opened the door he was more than a little surprised to see a young girl standing there. He had thought it might be DS Cummings, who felt he could pop round at any hour of day or night and often did, so he was quite startled to see a pretty young face looking back at him instead of the Sergeant's hawk-nosed countenance. He was even more surprised when she held out her hand politely and introduced herself.

"Hi Mr. Haley, It's Gemma, Gemma Cooke, I'm in your form class."

He shook her hand and stared at her, trying desperately to place the name and recognise her so as not to seem rude. She had confused him by saying she was in his form class, for he knew they were all first years and this girl must be at least thirteen or fourteen.

"Are you sure? I don't have a third year form class. Are you sure it's not English or Humanities?"

Gemma giggled at his mistake, which was fairly normal given the circumstances. He hadn't been at school for over two weeks now and he hadn't been there very long in the first place, plus the fact that she was well aware that she did look much older than her years. She had started developing breasts when she was nine and a half, and from there it had just escalated. It had been awful at first, being so different from her friends, putting up with all the embarrassing comments about how fast she was growing up. But she was used it now, and at times it was even fairly cool, having all the older boys fancy her and having fun telling them all to get lost. For Gemma had decided she did not have time for boys yet, she wanted to do well in school and get into a really good university so that she could become a doctor or a journalist or maybe just a teacher like Mr. Haley, so she could help other kids to become doctors or journalists. Gemma was clever at everything and could not make up her mind what career to choose, but despite what her body suggested she was still young, and at the moment all she wanted to do was get some answers.

"Yes, I'm sure," she said, still smiling sweetly, "I am a first year, I'm only eleven but I get that a lot, people thinking I'm older an' everything. Anyway, it doesn't really matter I just wondered if I can come in and ask you stuff." Richard still looked puzzled so she improvised quickly, "It's for a project I have to do. It's on trees and plants and things you find in a forest, only obviously we can't go in there but I figured you've been in there quite a lot so ..."

She trailed off, suddenly nervous and hearing the lie sound obvious and silly, but her teacher suddenly motioned her inside and without thinking she stepped over the threshold, fully realising her foolishness as she did so but unable to change her mind as he closed the door behind her.

"Everyone knows I'm here," she blurted, panicking, "I mean, my mum and dad and the school and everyone. They all know where I am."

They stood in the hallway and Richard stared at her again, recognising for the first time the reputation he had earned in such a short time. It saddened him deeply and he felt horrified at the awareness that this girl was actually frightened of him, a pupil who had previously trusted him now actually thought him capable of violence and savagery. He sighed and walked through into the kitchen, not knowing what to say to reassure the girl who stood motionless, still in the hallway, clearly staying within running distance of the front door in case he chose to pounce on her. So he just flipped the switch on the kettle and sat down.

"The door's not locked, Gemma. It is Gemma right?" She nodded, still nervous, "And if you like you can stay there and I can stay here because the last thing I want is for you to be scared of me, OK. I'm actually having a hard time coming to terms with the fact that you are scared of me but I suppose that's what you get for running around in the Blackhart right now isn't it?" She nodded again, with a brief smile this time, but she was still uncomfortable and Richard hated to see it. He had no idea what to do to make her feel better so he said the only thing he could think of which was true. "I'm your teacher, Gemma, I'm not the Blackhart Scarrer and I'm not mad either, despite what everyone else is saying. I'm just a teacher, OK? And I'll be back at school before you know it, you'll see." He tried a quick half-smile, designed both to charm her and to restore her confidence, which she clearly must have in abundance to be here in the first place. But she was still frozen in place, as if her feet were glued to the floor and her lips were glued together. He was running out of options but as he looked at her he realised he had gone about this in entirely the wrong way. He was her teacher, not a friend or a stranger, and he needed to behave like a teacher.

"Right Gemma, you've got precisely ten minutes to ask your questions and then I'll have to ask you to leave because I'm very busy." He made a show of looking at his watch, "Time starts now, young lady, first question please."

He looked at her sternly for the first time and she seemed to snap out of it, showing her true age by pulling a Simpsons notepad from her schoolbag with a matching pen. She paused for a moment, clearly pondering her question and then carefully replaced both notepad and pen into her bag and moved into the kitchen to sit beside him.

"I lied about the project thing," she answered glumly, "I'm sorry Mr. Haley, it's just that no-one tells you anything when you're my age, and, well, I thought you were a nice teacher and I didn't want to believe all that stuff but ... well ... it's just that ..."

"I know," he spoke kindly, cutting her off, "it's OK, I understand. But even though I'm not the bogeyman I hope you really did tell everyone where you were going because you really shouldn't be here." He was glad she wasn't scared now but at the same time he knew he had to impress upon her the extreme dangers of just walking into a man's house the way she had done, and he could not help but feel angry when she shook her head miserably.

"Jesus, girl!" He softened at the sight of her quavering lip and tried to calm her. "Listen, you've got nothing to worry about here but you had no way of knowing that. You barely know me at all and I'm sure you've been taught not to talk to strangers since you were a little kid, haven't you?"

"But you're not a stranger, you're my teacher!" Gemma looked defiantly at him and he grinned at her smart-alec attitude before continuing.

"Yes, but that doesn't make it OK for you to come into my house on your own, especially at the moment. In fact, you knew it was stupid the second I shut the door, it was written all over your face. So if you knew it was stupid why on earth did you do it? Why are you even still here now when we're having this conversation? Shouldn't you be running for the door at full pelt by now, just in case?"

The girl shrugged and while he was glad that she obviously trusted him again Richard was also concerned that she clearly hadn't got the message he was desperately trying to convey so he went on, trying to make her understand but at the same time not wanting to terrify her.

"I'm saying you should probably leave now, Gemma. It's lovely to see you and I'm happy you don't think I'm a monster anymore but you have to realise that one day you could walk into some other bloke's house and he really *will* be a monster, or it could be a woman for that matter. You just don't do it, OK?" He shook his head in disbelief as she finally muttered "yes Mr Haley" and stood up to leave. He was amazed at her courage but he couldn't shake the feeling that he hadn't said enough, that this beautiful girl would go through life like a cat, curiosity ruling at every point. He noticed Frankie playing on the stairs as he showed her to the door and decided that although the saying was corny, at this moment it was also apt and important. He picked up the kitten and as she turned to say goodbye she immediately crooned in delight and reached out to stroke him.

"That's my point, Gemma, you did it again." She looked back at him, totally confused, and blatantly annoyed that he had pulled the kitten away from her reach. "How do you know he's not going to scratch you or bite you?" He asked her, calmly proving his point.

She shrugged, looking at Frankie and unable to stop herself from smiling. "But he looks so cute. Look at him, he wouldn't hurt me would he?"

"No, he wouldn't, and now that you've asked someone responsible who happens to know him extremely well you may stroke him." Richard stepped forward so that she could reach the enticing black fur and they both smiled as Frankie began to purr loudly. After a minute she stopped and surprised him on the doorstep for the second time by seeming to read his mind, and he knew the message had sunk in after all.

"Curiosity killed the cat, huh?" She grinned one last time and walked away, saying very quietly, under her breath, "but I'm still alive, Mr. Haley, I'm still alive."

"And for God's sake don't go near the forest!" Richard yelled after her as she sauntered smugly down the street though he couldn't be sure if she had heard him. Unfortunately, he had not heard her last comment or he may have run after her, made his point more forcefully, made her swear not to go in there. But he just smiled and closed the door. The police said he may have been the last person to see her alive, other than the Blackhart Scarrer of course, but the insinuation was less than subtle.

**

At nine o'clock, when Gemma still had not arrived for registration or for her first class, the relief teacher who was filling in for Richard Haley informed the school secretary who immediately called Gemma's parents to find out if she was poorly or if there was any other problem. The school had become extremely strict on punctuality since the scarrings had begun and expected the parent or guardian of any child to inform them by 8.45 a.m. if their child would not be attending on that particular day. As no such call had been received from Mr or Mrs Cooke the secretary was mildly concerned but mainly just annoyed as she fully expected Gemma's parents to have simply forgotten the new rule. If she had known them at all, however, she would have been well aware that they were not the type of people to forget any rule or regulation and she probably would

153

have called the police first. But, unfortunately for Gemma, Miss Bell had never met her parents, so she phoned them at home and spoke to Mrs Cooke, who informed her politely but firmly that she must have made a mistake, that her daughter had left for school about an hour ago because she always liked to arrive early. Miss Bell was then forced to double-check with Gemma's teachers before calling her back, all of which wasted precious minutes, and by the time DS Cummings received the message that a normally extremely conscientious eleven year old girl had not turned up for school it was a quarter to ten. He already had two men patrolling the forest path, as usual, but when his team at the station were told they could have another potential victim on their hands they all wanted to help with the search. Before long the Blackhart was swarming with cops, again, and because it was a small town, everyone soon knew that another girl was missing, which is why Katrina found out when she popped down to the supermarket to buy some eggs for a very late breakfast.

"Richard?"

"Kitchen hon'. Did you get the paper?"

Katrina went through and plonked her shopping on the table, the newspaper Richard wanted clearly visible rolled up and stuffed haphazardly down the side of a bag against a carton of milk. He reached for it but Katrina grabbed his hand and pulled him towards her for hug so he wrapped his arms around her instead and asked if she was OK.

"Not really. I just heard in the shops there's another girl missing. I can't believe it." She sighed and tried to bury her head in his chest. "I guess I thought it would be over by now, that they'd have caught the bastard, or at least that no-one else would be stupid enough to go in that stinking place."

"Oh God." Richard drew away sharply and clenched his head in his hands. "Do they know who it is? When was it reported? Oh God oh shit!" The words tumbled out, frantic and angry, and Katrina looked at him strangely.

"They say it's the Cooke's little girl, no-one seemed to be able to remember her name, Jenny or Julie or something, but she's much younger than the others, just a child really, well, I suppose they all are aren't they." She trailed off, watching, disturbed, as he became more and more distraught until finally he blurted out: "Gemma, her name's Gemma. Jesus, it can't be. Shit shit shit!"

He moved past her suddenly and hurried through to the phone in the hallway. Katrina followed him.

"Gemma. Yes, that's it. What's going on Richard? Who are you calling? You're kinda scaring me now."

"The cops. Cummings." He punched in the number and waited, impatient as the phone caught up and began to dial. "She was here, for God's sake, this morning. Didn't you hear the doorbell?"

"Yes, vaguely, I was knackered." Then it sunk in, "Fuckin' Hell! She was in the house? Here? Today? Here?" Katrina began to pace restlessly, not comprehending. "But why? Why would she be here Richard? Oh my God are you sure it was her? Gemma Cooke right, not another Gemma, 'cos. there's that Gemma Cookson who lives just up the road y'know. Maybe you're getting mixed up." She stared at him hopefully but he shook his head and shushed her as the call was obviously answered. He asked for D S Cummings but clearly did not get to speak to him so he left an urgent message and within two minutes he was on the line and talking so fast the Sergeant could barely understand a word he was saying.

"You need to calm down Haley, I think. Yes, calm it

right down before you have a coronary, that's the ticket." He waited for Richard to take a breath as though he was about to speak and then continued at his usual relentless pace, making sure there was no chance for interruption.

"Right then. You say Gemma Cooke came to see you this morning? Yes. And she was asking you questions? Yes again. And then she left and then you said something about your cat. That's where you lost me I'm afraid. I don't honestly see the relevance of the cat episode but I'm sure you can explain and that's all very well but I think it would be best if we had this whole conversation again don't you? Yes. Good. Right then, I'll see you down at the station in about twenty minutes, OK?"

Cummings hung off without waiting for an answer and sighed loudly, shaking his head. Richard mirrored this action almost exactly, holding a dead phone and now too exasperated for his previous panic to remain. He soon realised, however, that that had been the Sergeant's intention and he could not help but smile at the man's clever use of psychology and at how well they had both got to know each other over the last few weeks. Katrina had only heard one side of the conversation, however, and was still reeling at the idea that a scarring victim had visited their house just before she was abducted. She knew that half the town already suspected that Richard was somehow involved in the scarrings and she knew what they would think if this became public knowledge. Frankly, the thought terrified her. Which was why his next statement chilled her to the core and she burst into tears.

"I have to go down to the station."

**

156

As Richard held her sister and told her that everything was going to be all right, Bethany held Gemma Cooke in a deep sleep and told her the exact same thing. She had been amazed to feel the child running swiftly through the forest earlier as the constant police presence had convinced her it would be a long time before anyone else set foot in her sanctuary again. So, obviously, she had gone to see who this courageous person was and had been even more amazed as she felt the girl's heart pounding fearfully and knew that she was far too scared to be here at all. Despite her fear, however, this brave and clever girl had managed to outsmart the policeman patrolling the entrance and Bethany grinned at the incredible audacity which, against all reason, had somehow succeeded in overriding that fear. Still, she was running quite fast and if Bethany wanted to catch her she would have to be pretty smart herself. Or maybe not. For as she watched, still smiling but becoming concerned now at the girl's obviously increasing terror, the running child tripped as she looked over her shoulder yet again and completely missed a giant tree root which lay directly in her path. She fell quite hard, badly twisting her ankle, and Bethany heard her frustrated yell of pain from quite a distance. Her basic instinct screamed at her to run and help but she held back, knowing she could not afford to be seen until she was close enough to force the girl into the deep sleep which she would need to make her safe. Because Bethany had noticed instantly how beautiful the girl was, and that meant she was in serious danger.

Gemma sat up, tears shining in her eyes, and brushed the dirt from her clothes before attempting to stand. Her sore ankle immediately gave way and she sat back down again, muttering "ow, ow, ow, bugger, ow, ow," under her breath repetitively, unaware that as she held her foot, rocking unconsciously, she was being expertly stalked, and that soon it would all be over. As she drew nearer, Bethany reached out and grasped gently for the girl's mind, first locating her name and repeating it softly and monotonously until her breathing deepened and her heartbeat slowed considerably. Gemma felt suddenly peaceful and the pain in her ankle disappeared. She felt as though someone was tenderly massaging her head from the inside out, but the confusion of this was quickly overpowered by an intense drowsiness which she could not resist. Bethany smiled sweetly down at her as she closed her eyes and curled up on the floor, head resting on the thick root which had caused her to fall in the first place. She was already fast asleep and Bethany was glad that this one called Gemma was so easy. She had not fought the sleep at all and as she stroked her cheek affectionately she forced her to rise up and stand beside her, still sleeping, so that she could guide her to a special place, a hidden place, where her face could be recreated with loving care to keep her safe from all mankind.

Bethany held Gemma's hand and walked her deep into the forest. They stopped at the foot of the Father Tree and as Bethany called upon the Blackhart to begin the scarring process two huge long branches bent down like giant arms and wrapped around Gemma tightly, carrying her high up into the canopy where yet more branches squirmed across her body until she was cocooned in a leafy embrace with only her face clearly visible amongst the greenery. Bethany leapt after her, scaling the gigantic tree as nimbly as a cat, and settled on a thick branch just below. She had to be near enough to hold the sleep throughout the scarring but she could not bear to watch. She had tried to watch with the one called Katherine, that first time, but it had made her queasy and strangely sad, so she had relegated herself

158

to the branch below and covered her eyes, hating the smell of blood and determined not to see the scarlet splashes which she knew were the dreadful accompaniment to that acrid scent. And, as she waited, she felt the spirits arrive - those whom she had not healed as a punishment for the suffering they had caused to so many others - the cuckoo, the grey squirrel and the crow. Powerless to resist her beckoning they came together, these three tortured souls whom she had banished from eternal rest and, as they began their terrible work, she kept Gemma's dreams serene and full of beauty; of sunshine and flowers and waterfalls, tranquil, happy and pure so the ripping claws and slashing beaks could not hurt her and the scars she retained would be only on the outside, where they would wreak the least damage.

During this controlled disfigurement, Bethany and the Blackhart breathed as one, lost in concentration and almost oblivious to their surroundings, which is why they were both caught by surprise at the sudden influx of people within the forest boundaries. The girl called Gemma was almost dropped, but Bethany was able to calm the forest quickly, knowing that they were far too high off the ground to ever be noticed, and knowing too that it was extremely unlikely that anyone would venture this deep into the forest's centre. Until herself, she was fairly sure that no other human had ever even seen the Father Tree and she soothed Elan with this knowledge until his grip tightened once more and the girl was safe. The problem now though, was that the scarring was almost over and it would soon be time to begin the healing, and Bethany could not perform that particular art without the soothing flow of water from the stream by her den. She knew she must act fast, as the hurrying, vengeful footsteps of dozens of policemen echoed through her head, so she cast the demon creatures away and willed Elan to lower the girl gently back to the floor where she could move her quickly towards the stream. Thankfully, they did not have far to go and, as she did not need the Blackhart's help in the healing process, she implored it to keep her hidden while she worked, to keep the frantically searching men at a safe distance so that she could finish what she had started, undisturbed and uninterrupted. She should have known, really, that she had no need to ask such a thing. For as much as the forest loved it's healer it hated the intruders, and the pretty glade where Bethany sat with Gemma to heal her face was soon invisible to all outside it, well protected with swirling winds and whipping ferns, cleverly concealing the waiting fangs of adders and the low but steady growl of thirteen foxes who encircled the area, patient in their distemper, knowing only that they must guard this area with their lives or face the wrath of their keeper, the Blackhart, which none would dare to do. The wild boar which had so terrified Richard was nearby too, snorting and stamping in anticipation, but the mist and the winds did their job too well, and the creatures did not get a chance to prove their loyalty - the men simply walked right past, unaware of the miracle taking place just a few steps away.

Bethany had ended the scarring sooner than usual, and as the girl's skin was younger and the girl's mind was so pliant, her job was much easier this time. She knelt over Gemma's body and moved both hands over her face, feeling the cuts and tears close up beneath her fingers, but making sure they closed in all the wrong places, overlapping and crossing and pinching, instead of joining smoothly together without leaving a mark, which she was more than capable of. But what would be the point in that. If she did that then the girl known as Gemma would leave with her face still pretty and perfect, and the world was not a pretty and perfect place, so Bethany worked her magic and left the once lovely face in a pattern of knots and creases and coils until it was as ugly as it needed to be to let her live free, free from the innate and terrifying dangers of her previous prettiness.

When it was over they just had to hide and sleep some more, until the darkness came to give them shelter for the long walk back to the path where the saved one could be allowed to wake in a familiar place. The glade was still under expert protection from the Blackhart so Bethany simply moved the girl to a shady spot and lightly camouflaged her body with bracken and ferns. She left her there, setting her brain to constant sleep and returned to her den, needing to rest before the journey later on. She did not mean to fall so deeply asleep but the hurried healing had tired her much more than she realised and within minutes she drifted off, breaking her grip on Gemma's mind far too early. It was a mistake which cost her dearly, and when she woke to the blackness of night the girl was gone. She did find her though, and she found her quickly, for the scent of death lay heavy in the air, and when she did she howled at the moon like a wounded wolf. It was a chilling, mournful sound for those who had the misfortune to hear it, and they glanced at one another furtively, hearts beating faster, palms sweaty, hairs pricking like needles. Outside the forest the night was clear and warm, inside it was cold and bitter, and as the rain crashed down it mingled with Bethany's tears and soaked the ground until the blood had disappeared completely, and she was left there alone, still wailing, still angry and trying to understand, keening in horror and pain at what she had caused, and aching, aching so badly she could barely breathe, aching with the agony of regret.

**

Hartsbridge Police Station was just outside the town centre and although neither Richard nor Katrina had ever set foot inside it they both knew where it was. It was one of those old buildings which had stayed in the same place for ever and hadn't really changed since it was built. Katrina had insisted on tagging along with her boyfriend and though, at first, Richard had been annoyed at her clinginess, by the time they reached the station he was very glad of the moral support, as from the looks he received once inside he felt he would be a trembling mess of a man if he had gone there alone.

DS Cummings was a friendly face amongst the black tempers and sullen expressions of his colleagues and the couple were only too happy to be shown into a private interview room where they could speak to him without so many angry stares. Now that Richard had calmed down he was able to describe the events of the morning with much greater clarity and the Sergeant took a full statement from him, seeming pleased at his awareness of times and the fact that Gemma was only in the house for a brief period. It was a short statement, which they were all happy about, as the chairs were of the uncomfortable plastic type and the room was small and borderline claustrophobic. But when it was signed and finished no-one stood up to leave and the silence became almost as uncomfortable as everything else. Finally, DS Cummings cleared his throat and Katrina opened her mouth, both at the same time, and it was Richard who spoke first.

"You do believe me? Don't you? I mean, I know what everyone round here thinks but I thought, well, I thought you would know me enough by now, y'know?"

The sergeant barked out a laugh and that answered

the question before he spoke. "Of course I believe you Haley. Of course, young man. When you lie you might as well write 'I'm lying' in big black letters on your forehead. Yes. Hopeless liar, Haley, that's you. No point at all in lying when it's so obvious, is there? No, of course not. So, believing you is not a problem when you tell the truth. The problem, Haley, the *big problem* is that I have a lost child out there - again - and this lost child just happened to pop round to see *you* before she went and got herself lost." He sighed and shook his head. "You, of all people. My goodness Haley, it does not look good now does it? No, not at all. I should keep your doors locked at night that's for sure, and don't even think about going back into the forest. Not ever, I shouldn't think, not until we have someone behind bars for this dreadfulness." He looked up and caught Richard staring off into the distance, clearly paying no attention to the Sergeant's warnings. He sighed again and glanced over at Katrina, who had her head down and was picking at her fingernails nervously. She felt his gaze and clenched her fists to calm her hands. After a deep breath she looked over at Richard and then back at Cummings. When she spoke it was with a tension he recognised as very close to panic and he found it impossible to comprehend how she could be so frightened when the fear was based purely on something she herself barely understood.

"My sister's in danger, Sergeant. Something terrible, I mean *really* terrible is going to happen. And soon. I can't explain it but you have to believe me. You have to find that girl, you have to find Gemma and then you have to find Bethany. Before it's too late for both of them."

She was pleading with him, the fear and insistence flashing forcefully from her eyes, but still he did not understand. He remembered her sister's disappearance all too well, remembered Katrina at the time, wild, hysterical, green eyes glinting with tears and with anger as the doctor stuck the needle in her arm. He remembered too the endless searching, day after day, finding nothing but sadness as they returned empty-handed, and he remembered hating the forest then almost as much as she did for concealing their quarry. Katrina had been the strong one though, not her mum, definitely not her dad, and Cummings had seen her gradually take over the running of the house, her parents slowly stagnating in each other's misery, their remaining daughter as invisible as her sister, as they mourned for Bethany with such devotion that they completely forgot the child who was still alive. And Katrina had never blamed them for the way they treated her. She had nursed her mother through the cancer which finally killed her and stayed at her father's bedside to patiently care for him as he slowly slipped away, dying more from a broken heart than from anything physical. And now, now that she had no-one left to look after, Katrina's rock of inner strength upon which she had built her life, her whole personality, was gradually deserting her, running for cover as the whole sorry mess was brought back to life with her boyfriend's ridiculous obsession with a Bethany look-a-like running loose in the very place in which the real Bethany had disappeared. Cummings felt sorry for her, felt sad for her, but he could not imagine what he was supposed to say to someone who had lived through something which he had only viewed from the outside. He took her hand in his and tried his best.

"I have lots of men out there, Miss Rose, good men. I know it's a cliché but we are doing everything we can, everything, to find the young Miss Cooke. As for your sister, I am thinking you must learn to say goodbye, my dear. It has been many years, has it not?

Yes, many years now, and I do not think we shall find her any more today than we did all that time ago when I was still in training and running through the forest with the boundless zeal that only the young possess." He smiled at the memory and Katrina took the opportunity to interrupt. She was not smiling, and her tone did not conceal her contempt for his condescending speech.

"Don't patronize me, Sergeant. I don't really care if you think I'm crazy but you could at least treat me with a little respect." She rose to her feet and addressed both of them, Richard now startled from his reverie by her indignation. "Now I don't give a damn what either of you think, I know for a fact, *one hundred fuckin' percent* that Bethany is alive and she's in that forest. Now maybe the girl Richard saw isn't her at all, or maybe it is and she's been living wild and she just looks a lot younger than she is. I don't know. And I don't honestly give a shit. But she's there all right, and I'm telling you that something awful, something cold and wrong and horrible is going to happen and whether you believe Bethany is alive or not isn't really relevant. Because it's not just about her is it?"

Katrina was shaking, her voice had risen about two octaves and all she wanted was for someone to take her seriously for once. That, and a cigarette. She was still smoking a little, though she was trying to cut back, but the pressure in her head was building every day and the same nightmare came every night, even through the brandy she tried to drown it with. Richard had been too wrapped up in his own forest nightmares, and in his daydreams of the barefooted girl, to notice just how little she slept, or how much she drank and smoked in the evenings to try and cope with the insomnia. He coped with it by simply popping another sleeping pill. While she drank brandy downstairs he lay in bed listening to the TV and waiting for it to kick in, wondering when she would start going out again, when she would finally leave him alone so he could go back into the Blackhart without upsetting her.

Now he realised that she was trying to cope with her own problems. That ever since she had shown him the picture of Bethany and he had exclaimed that she was the one, that she was the girl in the forest, Katrina had been battling with the past, and with the hope that her sister was not only alive but close by. But then the scarrings had begun and so the hope had been replaced by fear, and with everything else that had gone on with himself and the Blackhart it was all too easy to see how she had become so scared and so confused. He looked at Cummings and saw his thoughts reflected in the man's face, but he also saw something else, something he couldn't quite place but which may have been a hint of suspicion, and he was amazed to find the same idea in his own mind, so he pushed Katrina gently down onto her chair and crouched next to her, tenderly stroking a strand of hair behind her ear and kissing her cheek to calm her.

"What do you mean, sweetie? What else is it about?"

She looked at him incredulously, "Well, *you*, for a start! For God's sake Richard you're involved in this, don't you see? It's no coincidence that every time you go into that God-awful place something happens to you. And then the scarrings - they all started just after you moved here. And then, after everything, this kid turns up on your doorstep and becomes the next victim!" She was shaking again, and held his arm so tight he thought her nails would draw blood. "Christ, are you both so blind you can't see that something seriously strange is going on here. It's the Blackhart itself, I swear. That forest is an evil place and it won't stop until ... until ... I don't know. Until someone does the sensible thing and razes it to the ground."

Katrina let go of Richard's arm and breathed in and out heavily, deliberately calming herself whilst the two men exchanged glances. She pretended not to see the look which passed between them but she did see it, she saw it clearly and she knew what they thought.

"If you don't want to take me seriously that's fine. Because you'll both see I'm right, eventually, and you can spend the rest of your lives blaming yourselves for not believing me. And trust me, that kind of regret is not something I'd wish on my worst enemy." She stood up, smoothed her skirt and straightened her hair. "I'll be waiting by the car hon', OK?" And she left.

As the door clicked shut Richard and Cummings stayed quiet for quite some time, each pondering her last words and all that had come before. It was the Sergeant who broke the silence, returning to the business at hand as though nothing had happened, and they were both glad to be back on a level they could deal with.

"We will be needing to have another look around your house, Haley, you understand. I could get a warrant but I'm sure you won't force that will you? No, of course not. Nothing there at any rate is there young man? No, nothing at all, just like before."

Richard smiled, sighed and nodded all at the same time but just as he went to turn the door handle Cummings put a steadying hand on his arm and he stopped, knowing there was another question hanging in the air between them.

"Quite upset your Miss Rose, isn't she? Yes, very upset I think." He paused briefly, Richard staring at him expectantly, "I don't really know how to put this so I shan't mince my words, Haley. Do you think she's altogether stable? Do you think we should be searching Miss Rose's house instead?"

For once the Sergeant didn't answer his own questions and Richard shook his head, glum because he knew exactly where the older man was coming from, annoyed because he had expected more sense from such a good judge of character.

"No, and no." He replied quickly and harshly, "she's stressed out, that's all, and who can blame her. But she's not capable of doing harm, Sergeant, not to anyone or anything. So although I can sort of see your point, you'd be wasting your time just as much as you're about to at my place. OK?"

He looked directly into Cummings' eyes as he spoke and the Sergeant nodded when he had finished. Only once, but it was emphatic and he held Richard's gaze as he did so. They left the tiny interview room together and Katrina was still smoking as they reached the car which she was leaning against. Her look of defiance sent blatant hostility to them both and Cummings was very pleased to be travelling in another vehicle. Katrina was certainly one of the most beautiful women he had ever known, she always had been, but on this occasion he didn't envy Richard Haley one little bit.

**

They went through the house in about ten minutes. Cummings stood outside in the garden and drank coffee, Richard stood with him, and Katrina sat on the wall in the front garden, smoking an unlit cigarette. WPC Hamshere and DC Barlow moved quickly and efficiently through each room and returned to the Sergeant empty-handed. He sent them back to the station and finished his coffee, talking little and staring constantly into the distant trees of the Blackhart. He had expected nothing else from the search of Haley's house but he had expected some news from the team in the forest by now and as the time ticked on he became more and more anxious, fearing the worst for Gemma Cooke and fearing another intolerable session with his DI if she wasn't found before nightfall. He didn't blame the Inspector, after all, the case had no clues and no suspects, and though it had been National News since the beginning, it was now the most high profile case in the entire country, and jobs would be forfeit very soon if a result wasn't forthcoming. But what result? He had nothing new to tell his boss except Katrina Rose's novel idea that the Blackhart itself was responsible, which was sure to go down really well in their next meeting, he thought sarcastically. So he said his goodbyes to Haley and headed off down the garden to take the short-cut to the forest which Richard had explained to him. It was much quicker than he had expected and he instantly understood how easy it would be for anyone living on this street to bypass the main entrances to the Blackhart and move into the forest completely undetected. He himself had to walk for a good few minutes before meeting any of his colleagues and he immediately sent two men to search the pathways which led to all the houses in that direction. He met Hobbs as he wandered, too, shaken by the man's haggard condition and pale complexion. It was something he began to notice in all the DCs he met, a weary and wretched composure with a glimmer of dread in their eyes which seemed much worse in those he met as he moved deeper inwards. The reason became clear as he encountered the freezing fog and swirling winds which appeared out of nowhere at certain points in the search, and he was acutely puzzled by these bizarre weather patterns on such a warm spring day. He had heard all the stories before, of course, from the men who were knocked out by falling branches and tripped by the apparently shifting floor, but he had put it down to the lack of light in such a tree-crowded place, and to a touch of mass hysteria caused by the constant talk of witchcraft and sorcery which had always surrounded the case. It certainly was very mysterious, he didn't disagree with that, and the world's finest scientists were still at a loss as to how the scarrings were achieved, but Cummings did not believe in magic or in voodoo or in any ridiculous superstition and he refused to become embroiled in the nonsense he heard every day. However, after spending a couple of hours in the Blackhart that afternoon, he could fully appreciate how the rumours had started. The place seemed cold and unwelcoming, utterly different to the day he had followed Miss Rose, yet just as strange. Then it had been silent and serene, now it was fierce with unseen rustlings and buffeting breezes, raising a chill even in his sceptical bones and filling his head with shadows and images of destruction. All he wanted to do was to get out of this ominous atmosphere and back into the light, but just like his men he did not want to leave without the girl. For, if a grown man, a cynic like himself, could be so affected, then how would a child fare in such surroundings. A child with only a madman for company, cutting her face to ribbons while she lay unconscious and dreamed of waterfalls and roses. And that was another thing. How could every girl dream the same dream. That had bothered him all along and he shivered to think of it, such mild and pleasant pictures in their minds while their skin was tortured and torn. He wondered if Gemma was dreaming right now, if they were already far too late and her pretty features had forever been erased like the drawings on a blackboard. He wandered and he walked, not out of the forest as his heart beseeched him, but further in, searching and searching till his complexion was as pale as the rest of them, his eyes bitterly downcast, his lips curled in a snarl of frustration as the Blackhart grew steadily colder and darker and he realised what the rest of them had known all along: they weren't going to find a thing.

**

When Gemma woke up it was so dark she thought she had gone blind, and she spent the first few minutes panicking, trying not to cry and rubbing her eyes repeatedly to try and make them work properly. Once her breathing had calmed and her eyes began to adjust she was relieved to find that she wasn't blind after all, that it was just very very dark in the forest, and then she thought she had just been knocked unconscious when she tripped over. For the trip was the last thing she could remember, that and an incredible feeling of sleepiness unlike anything she had ever experienced. She stood up and tried to look around her but the darkness was extreme and it was then that it hit her. Her eyes had felt really strange when she rubbed them, sort of wrinkled and lumpy and peculiar, so maybe her eyes were part of the problem after all, maybe she had picked up an infection or something from all the leafy stuff she was laying on, maybe she couldn't see properly because they were swollen and sore. But they didn't feel sore. In fact, she felt completely fine, including her twisted ankle and she certainly remembered *that* hurting like hell when she had fallen. Suddenly she began to feel afraid, and her brain was taking her in a direction that she badly did not want to go in. She tried to stop thinking altogether and she tried not to care that her ankle was fine and that her eyes felt weird, but the more she tried, the more she thought about it, the more she thought about the scarrings, which was exactly what she didn't want to think about in the first place. She was only eleven, she admonished herself, and the scarring victims were all over thirteen, so surely she couldn't be one of them, it just wasn't possible, and besides, her face wasn't hurting at all, nothing was, she felt fine in every way and if she could just find her way out of the forest she could go home and look in the mirror and she would see that everything was OK, except maybe for a mild case of conjunctivitis or something.

But the problem was that she really couldn't see very well at all. It was darker than she could ever have imagined and she was too scared to try and walk in case she fell over or strode head first into the nearest tree and knocked herself out again. So she knelt on all fours and began to crawl instead, desperate to do something practical to occupy her mind, to stop it from constantly begging her to check her eyes again, to check her cheeks and her mouth and her nose, to feel the smooth skin beneath her fingers which would tell her that everything was OK after all, that she wasn't a victim of anything except a simple trip which was what you get for not looking where you were going. She felt the floor in front of her and inched forward hesitantly, longing for a torch. The ground was soft and springy, dry but not too cold and she could hear the faint trickling of water just to her left. She moved towards the noise until the tiny stream came into view and she reached down to touch it, suddenly feeling extremely thirsty, and wondering if it was clean enough to drink. The water felt clear and cool across her fingers and she sniffed her hand tentatively, detecting only a slight earthy aroma which was not unpleasant. She licked her fingers experimentally and found the cold, fresh taste as agreeable as the smell, so she decided that it was safe and scooped the gently flowing liquid into her mouth until her dry throat was soothed and her body was refreshed. She had been careful not to touch her mouth as she drank but while she was leaning over the stream a tiny streak of moonlight found its way through the canopy, and for a fraction of a second her reflection flashed up at her.

Gemma drew a sharp breath in and shrank back from the water's edge. She did not scream or cry, she simply sat, frozen with disbelief, petrified of the tainted reality she had accidentally spied. She had no desire to look again at the horror of that impossible reflection, but she needed to be sure of what she had seen, to know for sure that her face was the ruinous mess of her darkest fears - so she raised her shaking hands towards her head. As her fingers reached the space before her face she experienced a terrorised moment of indecision, where her hands were incapable of moving any further, and they hovered there for what seemed like a tortured eternity while her mind attempted to prepare itself for the unthinkable. Finally, though, they closed around her skin and in that first split second of touch the decision was made.

Gemma sat still and felt a strange calm settle over her. Clinically, her body had gone into such an extreme state of shock that her anguish could not display itself, her emotions had been temporarily disconnected as a damage limitation device, and she was completely unaware of the natural chemicals coursing through her body to create this peculiar state. All she felt was nothing. And as she sat there, numb, detached, she felt her mind set free, and the sensation was wonderful, like a wild bird released at last to fly towards the sun. Her body seemed to move without instruction, her eyes seemed to see with total clarity yet with no recognition from her brain of what they looked at. She walked upright, confident and casual, and returned exactly to the place where she had stirred from her slumber. She felt on the floor until she found her schoolbag, somehow convinced it would be there, and then she continued her walk, pacing steadily into the thickest undergrowth, scratching her hands and catching her clothes on a countless array of thorns and prickles. After a while she stopped quite abruptly and pushed her way into the centre of a spiky bush, seeming not to notice the tears in her sleeves and the fine trickles of blood running down her arms. She sat cross-legged on the floor and frowned in concentration as she opened her bag and rummaged for her pencil case. As she pulled it out her new Harry Potter novel came out too, dropping unnoticed on the ground beside her. In her pencil case she found her scissors, which were the sharp ones her dad had bought her especially for Art class. They seemed light and insubstantial in her hands and she let the pencil case fall to the floor as she opened the blades and pressed one of the cold metal edges to her wrist. She paused only for a moment before applying firm, even pressure to the stroke and quickly slicing her skin in a single, controlled motion which caused a sharp intake of breath but no other reaction. The second wrist was slightly harder, as she found it hard to hold the scissors in her left hand, but she made the second cut with the same detached composure, the pain a fleeting memory as she felt the warm blood flow from her body. For some bizarre reason she was suddenly acutely conscious of staining her clothes, and she held her arms out to the side, the need to stay clean resounding in her mind. She stayed like that for the first ten minutes, until her aching arms overcame her willpower and she let them fall, choosing instead to straighten her legs and lay down flat on her back, arms resting gladly on the leafy branches of the elderberry bush she had chosen for her death bed. The bush was stiff and uncomfortable, but Gemma ignored the irritations it caused her and stared upwards, trying to catch a glimpse of the stars as she began to drift. Somewhere deep in her mind, distant synapses fired in rebellion, trying to rouse her from the peaceful destruction she had wrought, but Gemma could not be roused.

She wasn't scared, this dying child with the ruined face. She felt no pain and she felt no misery. She had few thoughts about what she did, it was as though her actions were pre-programmed, automatic, and because of that she felt that it was right what she had done, that her life had been happy and carefree, that she couldn't even think of living any other way. So she just lay there and waited, barely noticing the life-force within her gradually ebbing away. Her heart continued to pump and her lungs continued to breathe, and as the drowsiness crept upon her she had but a brief moment of disorientation, when the panic gripped her soul like the flapping of a freshly caught fish and she wondered where the Hell she was and what the Hell she was doing. But the confusion was short-lived and the hypnotic state which followed was impossible to fight. The sleep overtook her body with the speed of a launching rocket and the ease of a drifting tide.

Twenty minutes later, Gemma Cooke let out a final gasp of air and came to an end. There were no dreams before she died and she did not suddenly wake with some dramatic last words. She simply slipped away into the abyss, leaving her pale, empty body behind in a flattened bed of twigs and leaves. Her blood stained the branches and seeped into the ground all around her, but when Hobbs stumbled upon the body, on Bethany's invisible direction, it was the book which provoked the pool of vomit which he heaved up behind a nearby tree. He had a niece who was crazy about J K Rowling, and to see those magical pages such a dark

175

and gruesome shade of rust was truly abhorrent to him. Normally a stoic man, he had not shed tears in a long time, but he shed them for Gemma that night.

21

Grieving

The following morning the sun rose in the sky as it always did and the people got up for work and drove their cars and switched on their radios and televisions. Everyone breathed in and out without choking, the earth continued to rotate and children went to school in the uniforms they so despised. Dogs were walked at dawn and some of their owners collected their faeces in small plastic bags, and some of them didn't. Cats were called in for their morning feed, budgies had their cage covers taken off and hamsters curled up in tiny paper beds and went to sleep. Men and women arrived at their desks and switched on their computers, checking their e-mail and wishing it was lunchtime already. Housewives enjoyed a lay-in, mothers changed nappies, babies gurgled and giggled or screamed for their milk.

Somehow, although she couldn't understand it, the world had not stopped and she was still alive. Incredibly, she was supposed to eat and drink and take air into her lungs and carry on doing all those little things you did when morning came and you're daughter was dead. And what was it exactly that she was supposed to do? How was she supposed to function in any way when her heart and soul had been so viciously torn away from her, when the whole reason for her existence was gone, lost in the night and never to return?

She sat there on the edge of the bed, already showered, hair washed, dressed and with her make up put on as if nothing had happened. She had gone through her morning routine like a robot, exhausted from the strain of not knowing, numb from the shock of finding out. But suddenly the irrelevance of it all had hit her like a brick and she had simply sat down, wondering why she should do anything, why anyone should do anything, furious with the world for still being there, knowing she could not speak for fear of wailing like a banshee and wishing she could think of the tiniest thing to do which was in any way worthwhile. But she couldn't. So she sat there on the edge of the bed.

And outside the birds sang in the trees and the leaves stretched ever upwards to catch the light.

**

When Richard ventured into town that morning to brave the outside world for the first time since his unofficial suspension he could not have imagined just how awful the reaction would be to his presence. Even before the fate of 'little lost Gemma' (as she had already been dubbed) was common knowledge, he received open glares of hostility or terrified half-glances from almost everyone he saw, and one young woman even threw an egg at him, raising smug smiles from passers-by who clearly agreed with her sentiment. It amazed him how so many people who had never even met him could be so incredibly judgmental and so vehement in their mistaken beliefs and, as he wandered down the high street dabbing at his egg stained jacket with a handkerchief, he wondered if any of them would bother to apologise when the real culprit was finally caught. He doubted it very much, but he did wish the police would hurry up and find the madman so that all their lives could return to normal once again.

Just as he was thinking about Cummings and hoping

he had been successful in his search for Gemma yesterday, he walked past the window of an electrical shop and saw the Sergeant's face duplicated in a dozen television screens. He quickly ducked inside the shop and stood with a handful of other shoppers who had stopped to see the latest update on the Blackhart Scarrings case. As Richard entered they moved away from him and closed together instantly, huddling into a protective group as far from him as possible whilst still in view of the televisions. But, as Cummings spoke, their furtive whispering ceased and they simply stared at the screens in stunned silence as he told of finding Gemma's body in the forest, her face scarred, her young life taken by her own small hand. The Sergeant himself was visibly shaken and, after issuing his short statement to the press, he refused to answer any other questions and disappeared amidst a flurry of uniforms as the journalists yelled after him in disgust. Richard stood and stared at the set for some time, his heart breaking at the loss of such a wonderful child. He wished now that he had not let her leave his house alone, that he had insisted on giving her a lift to the school gates, or that he had talked to her while they walked there together, instead of inviting her inside and then throwing her out onto the streets all by herself. He should have trusted his instincts more, he should have been more like Katrina and listened when his inner voice had warned him that she was in danger, that she needed protecting. But he had not listened, and now she was dead. He had failed a bright young girl who thanks to him would now never have the chance to become a bright young woman, and the guilt must have shown on his face for the group of men and women in the shop had transferred their stares to him and the expressions of sheer hatred in their eyes was impossible to miss-read. Richard almost ran from the shop and he kept to the fast pace all the way home, wishing also that he had listened to Cummings when he had told him to stay inside and keep his doors locked. He had thought that the Sergeant must be exaggerating, but from the murderous looks he was given on the journey home he knew that, if anything, the comment had been understated. In fact, he would not have been at all surprised to find a lynch mob outside his house on his return, ready and waiting with a horse and a hood and a perfectly tied noose.

Katrina too had feared the worst when she saw the special news bulletin and she watched anxiously through a gap in the curtains as Richard hurried down the hill, wondering what on earth had possessed him to go into town on today of all days. When he finally reached the front door she held it wide and locked it carefully behind him, throwing both the bolts across as well, though they had never used them before. Richard instantly went to lock the back door in the same way but she had already done it and he noticed then that all the curtains were drawn and she was trembling with the misery of it all.

They sat together on the settee, holding each other, each wanting to say something to make it better, neither speaking for fear of making it worse. Richard could not help his anger at the stupidity of those who had decided his guilt based on nothing but rumour and coincidence, but Katrina understood their suspicions and only pitied them for their lack of reasoning. She was so sad at Gemma's suicide yet for some reason she had not been surprised at the news and a bizarre sense of relief had followed it, as if the young girl's death had brought an end to all the horror at last. Of course, she felt guilty for feeling such relief and she knew she could not voice her perception lest she was thought to be involved or just thought to be mad, which was what her boyfriend believed these days. She had wanted him to stand by her, had expected him to understand after all his strange experiences lately, but he seemed more determined than ever to remain devoutly cynical, to ignore even the testimony of his own eyes, to reduce the very fabric of his nightmares to a rational expression of post-traumatic shock, which was complete crap as far as she was concerned. His description of events for each episode in the Blackhart seemed to change each time they were described, and anything which seemed inexplicable was explained away easily as a hallucination brought on by exhaustion and the fear of being lost, not to mention by all the crazy talk of witchcraft and magic which clearly must have burrowed their way into his subconscious only to resurface at times of vulnerability and apprehension. They had it all worked out, her boyfriend and the sensible Sergeant Cummings, and they certainly weren't going to listen to the ravings of a frightened woman who had visions of destruction and believed that her long lost sister had been miraculously frozen in time.

Katrina knew how it sounded, she wasn't stupid. She had a Masters in Psychology for God's sake, not that either of them knew about that. She had told Richard about her Business Studies degree, but he was totally unaware that she had studied Psychology at the same time, and had gone on to complete her Masters, and that she was currently working on a thesis for her PhD. So she knew how it sounded; and she could analyse it logically till the cows came home. But the fact remained that nothing remotely logical was going on here. And while she was sure that they seen the end of the scarrings now, she still felt that Richard surrounded by a dazzling aura of danger, and that Bethany was somehow connected to that danger, drowning steadily in a cold green sea, with waves the colour of compost.

It would not be long now, she thought, until Richard gave in to his compulsion to revisit the Blackhart, his quest for the 'barefooted girl', as he insisted on calling her, still burning so brightly in his veins she could almost see it, almost touch it, as she caressed the muscles on his arms with her fingertips. She knew it would be impossible to hold him back this time and she knew that for once she would not even try. Her plan of action was already in place and when the time came she would simply follow him. She would call Cummings first and then she would brave the forest for a second time, satisfied that since she had conquered her phobia once she could do it again. Especially if it was her only chance to keep him safe, this stubborn, irritating man she loved so much it sometimes felt like pain, so tangible was the feeling, so powerful and intense. She wondered why it had taken her so long to realise it, after all these years of holding back, of rejecting the monogamous ties which society demanded, and she could only assume that the thought of losing him had jolted her true emotions to the surface, so that she no longer cared about monogamy or morals or the differences between sex and making love which she had so rigidly adhered to. No, all she cared about now was Richard. And keeping him safe, and unhurt; loving him and being loved by him in a pure, unconditional sense which only a few weeks ago would have seemed like the nonsense of fairy-tales and American movies. Yet her protective streak seemed to have summoned these feelings from the hidden depths where they were buried, that and the memory of her love for Bethany, which had stayed with her through everything, solid and uncompromising. She had no idea how she was supposed to save her sister, or even if Bethany would allow her near enough to try, but she knew that she must at least make the effort. She had let her down so badly in the past because of her own selfish fears, that this time she knew she had to do something, and when the time came she fully intended to walk headfirst into the nightmare and fight for the only family she had left, to fight the whole forest if she had to, to fight for her kin, her little sister, her Bethany.

Katrina was terrified of what lay ahead, but she was committed to her plan and in a way she hoped it would not be too long now, for the tension of waiting was only building her fear, just as the anticipation was gradually growing in Richard, until they both seemed ready to burst at the slightest flicker of light through the treetops. They stayed close over the next few days, but spoke very little, and when the day of the funeral arrived they both knew it would soon be time. Out of respect, Richard had decided to wait until Gemma's memorial service was over before he returned to the forest, and Katrina had picked up on that straight away, especially as his entire demeanour changed that morning, and she wondered if he would be able to wait even one more day, or if he would succumb to temptation and head out the moment it was over. She hoped he would choose to wait just that little bit longer, that he would set out in the morning with hours of daylight ahead instead of forcing the darkness upon them, when the Blackhart would be in its element and they would be left half-blind and defenceless, lost amidst the treacherous woodland, stumbling around like new-born calves with no mother to guide them safely under her flanks until the storm passed.

Watching him dress in his darkest suit and sombre-est tie she felt a rush of love for him which flooded her senses and drew tiny puddles to the corners of her eyes. She was amazed at his courage in attending the service and refused to feel frightened at the thought of being with him. Instead she would feel proud, proud and sad for them all, that they could not see the wonderful man at her side, that they did not know the true Richard Dean Haley as she did; a kind and gentle man who cuddled his kitten when he thought no-one was looking, a man who said sorry if his passion caused him to be even the slightest bit rough in bed.

Katrina chose an elegant black dress with a burgundy wrap and matching shoes. Her green eyes shone and her dark hair floated and they would all *say* she looked like a witch but they would all *think* she looked beautiful and what they would remember was how she clung to her boyfriend, how she wiped away silent tears and how she looked up at him with an expression of such love and trust that they wondered if they were wrong about him after all.

Richard waited until it was over. He endured the filthy looks and the caustic comments in hushed but scathing tones, and when they walked home he announced that he was going for a "quick run" to "clear his head and work off the frustration". Katrina just nodded her response and so caught up was he in the throes of his obsession that he did not even notice her easy acceptance. His mind was focussed only on the forest, on the girl, on the sweet release from the torture of waiting and waiting and waiting some more. He wasn't going to wait any longer. It was time.

**

On the day of her daughter's memorial service at St Peter's church, Patricia Cooke nearly got her wish. The world could not come to a standstill but, for that one morning, the town of Hartsbridge pretty much did. Schools were closed for the day, shops didn't open and practically everyone took the day off work. The town turned out in force to mourn the passing of one of its children, and the church was too small to hold such a huge congregation. They crowded the aisles and stood in droves against the walls, spilling out of the doors and forming broken lines in the courtyard, causing a silence so deafening that the minister himself had trouble speaking and the crack in his voice did not go unnoticed by the teams of reporters who had gathered at the side in a failed attempt to be unobtrusive. No cameras were allowed inside the church, but the press had not been banned from the event and they flocked to the scene like vultures, anxious to be part of the UK's biggest story since the Tube-Tazer - a disturbed teenager who liked to electrocute grey-haired business men on their way to work.

The service did not begin until ten thirty, but they started arriving as early as nine and, by the time Kathcrine, Zoe and Trinity turned up at precisely ten o'clock, there was already a large crowd. The three girls now went everywhere together and the community had grown used to seeing them now and again, always wearing different masks, always talking quietly to each other, always holding hands. They had refused to go back to school because it would mean they could not be together, but they seemed happy enough to learn at the same level with a private tutor which Katherine's father had hired. He was a good man, and did not mind that the other girls' families could not afford to split the fees, so he accepted whatever they offered and assured them that the friendship they shared was much more important than the cost, which was true, and in time all three families became almost as close as the girls themselves. It was still difficult for all of them, but the 'scar sisters', as they were happy to be known, were strong in their kinship, and their supreme show of courage at Gemma's memorial was a tribute to the unstoppable human spirit which blazed in their eyes and left a trail of burning embers in the hearts of all who saw them. Because, incredibly, they paused before they crossed the threshold to the house of God, and, as one, they removed their masks, clasping tight to each other's hands and moving forward with a prevailing dignity which entirely overcame the scars they wore. They had prepared themselves for gasps and screams and awkward mumblings, but instead they were greeted with stunned awe and a hushed respect which eased their misgivings and soothed their distress. The service was bitter sweet, poignant and passionate, and they cried for the younger sister they had never met, understanding her plight and seeing in each other's expressions that it could so easily have been any one of them, that she had spoken for them all when she had told the world that she couldn't possibly live like this, that it was just too hard to go on.

A lot of people cried that day and Gemma's mother was warmed by such compassion, by the endless stream of kind words and sympathetic hugs from her friends and family. She felt sorry for them all, in a way, knowing how difficult it must be for them too, how strange it must be to try and think of something to say which didn't sound incredibly lame in the face of her loss. But she also wished that she was one of them; that she could go home and say "that poor woman, losing her only child in such a way" and be secretly glad that it had happened to someone else and not to her. So although she answered them all with thank yous and politeness, she knew that this day would soon be over for them, that tomorrow they would go back to work and go back to their lives and that today would just be a small sad memory which quickly faded from their minds. While for her it was another day in Hell, with many more to follow, and as they all filed past her with their sympathies and words of wisdom, some with tears in their eyes, some still openly crying, she saw that they each wanted to ask the same question: 'Why aren't *you* crying? How can you stand there so unmoved and so calm when everyone else is so shaken and upset?' And she had no real answer to that. Except to say that if she started to cry she felt sure she would never stop. That the agonised screams which erupted from her throat would shatter the delicate stained glass windows and cause injury to any passing dogs, that her tears would flow like Niagra until the whole world drowned in the flood. And perhaps she would also say that she was saving her grief for a time when she would be able to cope with it much better, whenever that might be, and in her naivety that is what she really believed. But after about a month she finally realised that there would never be a time like that, that she would have to spend the rest of her life not really coping at all, that she wasn't actually expected to cope, that it was OK to scream and cry until she choked, to keel over as the pain seared her soul over and over again with an intensity which terrified her almost as much as it hurt. The fool who once said that 'time heals all wounds' was shown to be a dreadful liar, and, years later, when a newly bereaved friend asked her when it would get easier she was unable to reply, and the tears which streamed down her face answered for her.

**

Bethany sat behind the tall elm which marked the clearing and stroked Chaver's head gently. Since waking that morning she had sensed a subtle shift in atmosphere which told her that something important was happening, that a huge amount of energy was being focussed in one place, and she knew, therefore, that the forest would be subdued and reticent today, respectful of the unusual undercurrent of power filtering through from its human neighbours. She was glad of the quiet this produced, of the natural feeling in the air and the relaxed environment she could walk around in. Especially since the tension of the last few days had taken such a toll upon her. The crying she had done over the death of the girl named Gemma had lasted for hours and when she had finally stopped she had cried again, until she felt she had no more tears left inside her at all, that if anything else happened to upset her she would be unable to react, because her lifetime supply of teardrops had been used up and her eyes would be forever dry, forever swollen and sore, scratching her sockets each time they moved. She had not expected such a reaction and it had torn her apart that the one called Gemma had not understood. She had thought that all the girls would understand. She had thought it would be obvious to everyone that she had saved them from something much, much worse; she had thought they would be happy, that they would silently thank her and be glad to feel so safe in their new-found ugliness. But maybe she had been wrong all along. Maybe other people didn't think like her. Maybe some girls actually enjoyed being pretty and were perfectly happy with the type of attention their prettiness gave them. But she could not comprehend that part in the slightest. She could see why it was nice to look at a lovely reflection, to have people smile back at you when you smiled at them, but what came after the smiling was not worth what came before, and she wondered why the last one had not known that, why she did not realise that her lovely reflection would only destroy her as surely as the scissors she had chosen to do the same job.

So Bethany had not understood the death she had caused, but she had mourned it nonetheless and, though she had tried her best to breathe life back into the body, the spirit of the girl named Gemma had already flown away, and her efforts had been in vain. And when her guilt and her crying had finally gone away too, she knew that there would be no more scarrings. To cause a death, however unintentional, was a bad thing to do, a wrong thing, and she could not risk choosing another girl who did not understand, who held her vanity like a sacred prize inside her lifeblood so that the one could not exist without the other. Instead, she had decided that it was time to end it; to end everything, so that she could rest at last, with no more confusion, no more fear or pain or exhaustion but only peace and the pulse of the forest all around her; so much life, so much harmony and the simple pleasures of pure existence without any worries, without having to think at all. It would be strange, she knew that, but after all this time it would also be welcome, and she knew exactly what she needed to do to make it happen.

22

Remember

Bethany went to the clearing and waited. She called Chaver to her for she did not want to be alone when it was over, and he trotted up out of the bushes, as though he had been nearby all along, expecting her to need him at any moment. After a while some of the other creatures came to her as well, the injured hare who still had a slight limp, and the tiny dormice she had recently saved. Others arrived too: a squirrel she had healed years ago when he had lost half of his tail to a fast moving terrier who had slipped his lead, and a beautiful Great Spotted Woodpecker she had been forced to hand-rear after it's mother had rejected it by flinging it from her nest. She was very surprised to see them all, but not displeased, and they gave her comfort as she waited, each showing affection in their different ways, nuzzling and nibbling and nudging against her as she crooned to them softly with her velvety voice. Quickly they came, and, as Richard's first steps were felt in the Blackhart's soil, quickly they fled, until only Chaver remained at her side, knowing somehow that she must not be alone, that he must stay by her side until she asked him to leave and, even then, he would not go far, for he too felt a change was in the air and he would watch over her now as she had watched over him so many times before, until it was over, until they were both free at last.

When Richard reached the clearing she was standing there in full view, still and straight, eyes bright with challenge, a small, ragged fox growling almost inaudibly by her side. She touched Chaver's head lightly and as he sat down obediently the noise disappeared and Richard's apprehension left him completely, which was her intention. Then they just stared at each other for a long moment, Richard with awe in his face, with relief and anticipation, Bethany showing cold defiance, with a hint of welcome acceptance as her lips curled upwards at the corners. He was ready for her to run, to dart off suddenly as she had done before, so when she walked towards him and offered her hand he was too stunned to take it. He just stood there, dumbstruck, as she took hold of his fingers in her small smooth palm and pulled him after her, not running but strolling slowly and delicately through the undergrowth like father and daughter on a leisurely woodland walk. Richard just let her lead him onwards, and only when they had been walking for about half an hour did he try to speak to her.

"Is it OK if I ask you something?" His voice was low and breathless, tentative, not wanting to scare her off, and when he saw her nod he finally realised that she was not going to run away this time, that he was actually going to find out who she was and how she knew his name, that this really would be everything he had been waiting for. And as the excitement buzzed through his body she felt a familiar tingling in his hand and she almost screamed as she let go, the feeling was so powerful. His heart dropped as she released him and they both stopped for an instant as she almost fled, as he almost lost her yet again. But she forced her feet to remain steady and he breathed out in relief as she stayed at his side and beckoned him forward, no longer holding his hand for fear that the tingling sensation would return to panic her once more. Richard needed no encouragement to follow and he stepped up to walk beside her as they set off into the dense wilderness of the Blackhart, moving closer to the centre with every stride. He felt sure that she wanted to show him something important, that when they got there she would explain everything, but there was just one thing he wanted to know that he did not have the patience to wait for.

"I know you know my name, but I don't know yours. Who are you?"

Bethany didn't miss a step, though her heart skipped a beat, and she turned to face him as she answered, eyes flashing fiercely at his puzzled expression.

"You should know, Richard Dean Haley, but you don't remember."

His bewilderment increased and he frowned at her, wondering why her glare felt like daggers through his skull, and as she continued she turned away, walking faster now, the rangy fox trotting to keep up.

"My sister remembers my name, and you know my sister. My sister who loves you, and whom you love. She is with us even now, I can feel her, and she can feel us both. We must hurry, Richard Dean Haley. You know my name."

She spoke in one fluid exhalation and her voice melted in the breeze like ice in a furnace. Richard, shocked but not surprised, whispered "Bethany" as he fell into a sloping run beside her and, as the impossible reality sunk into his mind, he began to catch glimpses of the past and he wondered if he had known Katrina's sister after all, perhaps when they were kids, because he hadn't really known Katrina back then, so he would have had no reason to associate the two girls at all.

Then it struck him, the rest of what she'd said, and he asked her what she meant about Katrina being with them, being able to feel them, but she just shushed him and kept on running. So on he ran, deeper and deeper into the Blackhart, until they came to the silver stream which he tried not to recognise and beyond that an enormous oak tree which emanated strength and supremacy in a way that no form of vegetation should ever do. They stopped, and Bethany motioned for him to stay still while she drifted over to the giant tree and pressed her whole body against it, murmuring a muffled liturgy into it's darkened trunk. She was asking the forest for help just one last time, for her powers alone were not sufficient for the task ahead, and she needed it to go smoothly, to be a perfect re-enactment of the past which would finally show the impatient man who stood behind her what had happened all those years before, when she had run from bitter words which stung her heart to the sanctuary of the trees she loved, only to find that there were worse things than words to hurt her, that in her haven lurked a danger she had never imagined, one which she would never escape from.

As soon as the sap oozed beneath the bark and Bethany felt it's comprehension, the Blackhart began to darken and the girl moved back from the Father Tree, beckoning the man to follow her once more. She ran fast through the forest now, ducking and weaving as the darkness fell, leaving Richard far behind and leaving the beginnings of fear in his belly, for the day was still young and he guessed that the skies beyond the forest were bright with sunshine. But the girl stayed fixed in his sights and he ran with abandon, skipping over roots and brambles alike as she bounded gracefully ahead, fuelling his amazement with every elegant leap and agile gesture. In what seemed like an incredibly short space of time he recognised where they were, and he stopped in his tracks as the forest's exit drew near, feeling suddenly exhausted and wondering why she had brought them so close to the school and within easy sight of a bored looking policeman, should he but turn their way for a second. And then, right at that moment as he stared at him nervously, the uniformed man disappeared and he was seventeen again, weaving drunkenly past the school path and up towards his house on Wicksly Road.

**

It was a cold, damp night and Richard felt sick. He had been to a party at his friend Will's house, aka Wild Will, the guy who could 'get', the guy who everybody loved, who made a fortune by buying in bulk and selling in tiny one gram wraps or baggies of an eighth or sometimes even a quarter - for the hard-core stone-heads only, of course. They were teenagers and it was the start of the nineties, when drugs were cool and alcohol was boring, so everyone drank water and skinned up, snorting low-grade speed or charlie with a rolled up twenty off the toilet lid. Richard was too skint to buy any Coke himself, but he'd skagged a line off one of his mates and spent the rest of the night trying to pretend that the two grams of whizz he had been able to afford was really just as good anyway. The only problem had been when they had passed the joint around and he took a long deep puff of what he thought was just nicotine and hash, but what was actually some very expensive, extremely potent skunkweed, thrown in for free by good old Wild Will, the guy who everybody loved. Richard managed to keep his cool for around two hours, and then he forced himself to admit that if he smoked any more he would probably pass out, or worse, throw up on Will's mum's carpet, which would be particularly unpleasant for her to have to clean up in the morning. Ever the thoughtful friend, Richard decided to call it a night, and figured the fresh air of a long walk home would work wonders for his sobriety if his parents had not been sensible enough to go to bed before his return.

He had found himself in the forest a short time later, wondering how he got there and why. He vaguely remembered the party and feeling dizzy, but he also had the impression he was with someone, that his girlfriend Debbie was supposed to be with him, that he had lost her and she would be fuming, not to mention terrified, for she was scared of the dark and would never enter the Blackhart unless the sun was shining.

"Debbie?" He yelled, stumbling and reeling in circles. "Deb? Oh Debra darling, where are you?" He giggled at his singsong alliteration and moved deeper amidst the trees, completely disoriented but determined not to leave his girlfriend all alone in the darkness. Then he began to wonder if he had been with her after all, but he really hoped she was around because all that whizz had made him horny, as usual, and he couldn't stop thinking about her plump, round breasts which he loved to watch bouncing gently when she danced. He felt his cock stiffen as the image arose in his head and it was then that he saw her, a young girl dressed in an old-fashioned flimsy night-dress, white and flowing as she ran, eyes glistening with tears, hair loose and tussled around her shoulders. She ran towards him, oblivious of his existence until she was almost upon him, and he caught her neatly as she tried to side-step away. Deep in lust, in his drug-induced delusions, he saw her as a vision of his own creation, a nymph of the forest, a fairy or an elf sent to tempt and seduce him as he searched for his missing lover. Filled with false confidence, filled with passion, he introduced himself by bowing before her, a flourishing act, utterly ridiculous and the vision laughed as he spoke his name.

"Richard Dean Haley, at your service. And pray what is your name, oh sweet flower of the forest?"

The girl, who was younger in her mind than her

body portrayed, was delighted by his charming foolery and ceased her giggling just long enough to answer him.

"Bethany," she said, in a voice as clear as fountains, "Bethany Rose."

**

Katrina waited until she heard the back door swing shut and then she pounced on the telephone and made her call. Thanks to Richard, she had Cummings' mobile number and he obviously had their land-line programmed into his handset because he clearly expected her boyfriend to be on the other end of the phone.

"Haley. How are you Sir? Very busy this end so make it quick man, that's the ticket."

"It's Katrina Rose, Sergeant, I won't waste your time. I just need you to know that Richard went for one of his 'runs' in the forest a few minutes ago and I'm going after him. So if we both disappear you know where to look. That's all."

She didn't wait for a response and put the phone back in its cradle immediately. She had no idea what Cummings would do but she knew that if anything happened he would be the only person likely to understand and not to panic, so she trusted her own judgement in telling him and went upstairs to change. She dressed in green khaki and tied back her hair, a vague idea for camouflage which made her feel like she knew what she was doing. But she was still scared, and when she looked in the mirror she did not see the woman she had become, she saw only a frightened little girl staring back at her, eyes wide in her pale face. She took a deep breath and jumped as the phone rang. She knew it was only the Sergeant so she ignored it and went into the kitchen. Standing before the door she forced herself to calm down and count to ten, but by five she was too flustered to carry on and she stormed out into the garden instead, using her fear to fuel her determination. Richard had a good ten minutes on her and she knew that she had no hope of catching him, so she just hoped that her sixth sense would be as keen as the last time and she would simply walk right up to him again. Only, this time, she planned to reach him before anything bad happened, at least, that was the idea, and as she reached the garden gate she began to jog slowly, repeating their names likes a litany under her breath to boost her confidence.

"Richard...Bethany...Richard...Bethany...Richard...B ethany..."

Clearly, though, it was not having the desired effect, and by the time she came to the forest's entrance she was trembling and gasping as she tried to continue the chant. She had to force her legs to keep moving and once she was inside she felt a deep calm settle upon her just like before. Suddenly it amazed her that she had been so scared, that she hadn't remembered how peaceful it was in here, how beautiful and sweet the air smelt, how fresh and clean everything looked. She searched for Richard in her mind and centred on him instantly. He was happy but mildly frustrated, she felt, and she wondered what she was doing here, why he would need protection in such a wonderful place, and so she searched for her sister instead, and found a ribbon of destruction curling all around her, lashing out from her soul with dangerous precision towards a prey too full of excitement to notice. And then, shocked and confused, she saw that the prey was Richard, and she quickly remembered why she was here.

Katrina began to run. Slowly, of course, for her fitness regime consisted solely of eating very little and having plenty of energetic sex, but it was still a run, and after about forty minutes she realised how impressed she was that she hadn't collapsed in a coughing fit or just plain collapsed. She decided that maybe this fresh air and exercise thing really was good for you after all and thought she might ask Richard if she could go running with him now and again, if he didn't mind taking it easy so she could keep up, that is. However, just as she was congratulating herself on how well she was coping with both the forest and the running, somebody dimmed the lights, and the Blackhart grew dark with no warning. She checked her watch and wondered if a storm was brewing, as, according to the time, they should still have hours of daylight ahead. But she could not see the sky for the trees and for the darkness which hovered around her, tangible and cold, and as soon as the thought of a storm had entered her mind, it left again. This was no storm - this was the Blackhart. It had started already.

She quickened her pace and wished she hadn't cancelled her gym membership last year, not that she had ever used it, but she somehow felt that just by being a member she would be fitter, she would be able to breathe properly and her legs wouldn't be aching so much. But she didn't stop. She raced on through the darkness, following her feet and ignoring the signs of fatigue which coursed through her body. Her mind was locked on Richard and Bethany together now and she finally knew for certain that her sister really was the barefooted girl that her boyfriend was so obsessed with. She had known it was true but until that moment she had not truly believed it and, as she came upon the strange silvery stream which sprang from nowhere and flowed into nothing, she knew what Richard had never guessed: that she was entering the heart of the forest. And she also knew that here all things were possible, that reality could be toyed with like a mouse in a lion's den, that the Blackhart's will would rule in this place and that none of them should be here at all.

The powerful aura of her sister swarmed her senses as she moved through the long grass beyond the stream and walked carefully towards the voices she could now hear. She felt Bethany's awareness of her presence, and also her acceptance, but she sensed she must be quiet now, that there were forces at work which must not be disturbed. When she saw Richard laying still at her sister's feet she almost ran to him, almost broke the spell, but Bethany grasped her mind and froze her feet in place, until she sat, calm and ready, and let her mind be overtaken in a flurry of leaves and dazzling blue petals, which drifted across her eyes to wake her.

She was still in the forest but not in the same place. Her sister was walking hand in hand with a younger, quite drunken-looking Richard, and as they laughed she realised suddenly that her body was invisible, that although she could see them, they could not see her, and she knew then that she had not actually moved at all. Her body was sitting still where she had left it and if she wanted to go back she had only to reach for it with her mind and she would be there. So many times she would wish she had done just that, but she did not. Instead she chose to watch, to delight in the vision of her sister, happy, alive, and once she had started to watch it was already too late, it was too difficult to tear her eyes away and wrench them all back to the present. So she watched them walk, Bethany like a ghost in her white night-dress, Richard like an immature, inebriated Prince Charming. She was amused by it all, at first, before she noticed the look in his eyes and realised that he wasn't drunk, as she had thought, but that instead he was gone completely, a stranger in his place, a primeval specimen of a man who had no idea whatsoever of what he was about to do. She saw it before he did and though she tried to turn her head away she watched it still, and the unwanted image spun circles in her mind to make her dizzy, to make her sick, and as she forced herself back within the confines of her body the poison poured forth from her mouth until there was nothing left. Until Bethany came towards her and she stared up at her baby sister with a heart full of torment.

**

"Well, Bethany Rose, I was right, you are a flower. A pretty white rose blossoming before me. Will you walk with me my pretty rose? For I am lost and lonely in the dark, and I need your light to guide me."

Bethany was charmed by his old-fashioned speech, by his easy compliments and relaxed manner. The laughter bubbled up from her mouth like frothy water from a mountain spring, and she walked with him gladly, recognising those bright blue eyes instantly, though she knew she would never dare to voice her recognition. Of course she knew who he was. He was Richard Haley, he was 'the one'. There's one in every school, in every town, the one guy who everybody likes, who has all the best friends, who can go out with any girl he fancies and generally does, much to the envy of all the other girls. And then, of course, there are those who can only dream of being with him. They are the young girls, two or three years below, who see him for only fleeting moments, as they pass him in the hallway and sigh, wishing he would look their way even for a second, knowing that if he did they would just melt under his gaze and never recover. This was the Richard Haley she was walking with now. Richard Dean Haley. And he had called her his pretty rose.

Bethany, already half in love from afar, fell deeply

200

at that moment and would have walked with him to the ends of the earth if he had asked her to. But Richard had other things in mind. He wandered through the trees with his flower nymph beside him and revelled in the beauty of the forest and the mystery of the night. He watched the graceful movement of her lithe and supple body and he captured the delicate rippling sounds of her voice in his head. And as they walked and he talked and she lilted her responses he quickly noticed that their voices had become muffled to him, that he had no clue as to what was being said, that he did not want to speak any more anyway.

And suddenly he was upon her. The night-dress torn and flung up over her head as he groped at her breasts and kissed her body brutally. Bethany tried to scream, but all he heard was gentle murmurings, and in his twisted brain her frenzied struggling became writhings of passion and pleasure. He held her fragile body easily with one hand as he took down his trousers and freed himself, but as he forced himself inside her he moved the dress away from her head, so he could see the lovely face gazing up at him. Somehow her tears and her terror were invisible to him, and he smiled as he thrust within her, which is when she stopped fighting. For the smile did not belong to him, it was straight, symmetrical, nothing like the famous half-smile which had charmed them all, and as she stared up at him in horror she knew that it was no use. It was happening, it was hurting, it was tearing her apart but there was nothing she could do. So she lay still, and prayed for it to end.

For Bethany, the fear, the pain and the unbearable humiliation went on for what seemed like a lifetime. For Richard, the fun was finished all too fast. He grunted at the end and rolled off her quickly, staring up at the canopy of branches swaying him to sleep.

Bethany just wrapped her ruined night-dress around her ruined body and ran away.

**

As Richard lay sleeping both in the past and in the present, Katrina took her sister's hand and pulled her close, the taste of vomit still fresh in her mouth, her cheeks damp and her heart thudding with love and with horror. Bethany returned the embrace with a happiness she had no prior experience of, and they were both too choked to speak until the moment passed. As they broke the hug Katrina was first to end the silence, and once she had begun the words tumbled from her lips and she found it was almost as hard to stop talking as it had been to start.

"I'm so sorry Bethany. I'm so sorry. Really, I don't know what to say. I always loved you, you know? I still do, so much. I was such a stupid cow back then, I mean I really was and I'm sorry I was so mean and I'm sorry about all this, God, I had no idea, I mean I just can't believe it, Richard? God I'm gonna be sick again, sorry, I just.. God.. Bethany..oh God.."

She heaved into the bushes again but there was nothing left inside and the dry retching seemed to go on for ever until her sister placed a warm hand on her belly and another on her throat and suddenly she was fine again. An incredible feeling of tranquillity infused her senses and she stared at the young girl beside her with a mixture of awe and confusion.

"What did you just do? I mean, thank you, but...well.. did you just do something to me?"

Bethany smiled, sweet and serene, but as she opened her mouth to speak a lump rose in her throat and she had no breath to answer with. She wanted so badly to sit and talk with her sister, to try and explain why she hadn't been able to come home, to tell her that it was OK, that she had always understood the love they shared despite the shouting and the angry words, to tell her that she had been, and was still, the only person she missed every day, the only one she wanted to be with. But somehow she was unable to make the words appear and instead she simply squeezed Katrina's hand, trying to convey everything at once in a bizarre yet meaningful expression which her sister interpreted only as an inability to speak right now. Bethany led the older woman to Elan, the Father Tree, and motioned for her to sit down. She touched her eyes, pointed forwards and then gently closed her eyelids, still grasping her hand, inviting her to be calm, to watch, to understand, and in an instant she transported them both back to that terrible night, when she had left Richard fast asleep and run through the forest indiscriminately, wanting only to escape and forget and to pretend that nothing had happened.

They watched together as she ran and ran, her bare feet cut to shreds, her body bruised and sore, blood stains on her thighs, sticky and offensive like the semen it was mixed with. She ran until she could run no more, until her tiny lungs could no longer cope with the increased demand for oxygen, and she fell in a heap on the floor, bashing her head sharply on the thick root of a large oak tree which left her dazed and disorientated in the midst of her pain. When she managed to raise her head at last, she felt as though the ground had shifted beneath her, as though she had awoken in a different universe entirely, for she could hear the waters of a small stream babbling close by, and the moonlight shone as she had never seen it before, lighting up the leaves all around, and showing her a brand new world, a world more beautiful than she could ever have imagined. She stood and walked to the stream, marvelling in the silver water which ran through it, and without a thought in her head she was suddenly naked and splashing the clear warm liquid all over her body, cleansing herself with frenzied abandon in a brook which she knew could not possibly exist, but which soothed like silk upon her skin. When she was done she washed her night-dress too, needing to obliterate any traces of what had gone before, but then she realised she must surely be dreaming, for her skin and hair were dry the moment she stepped onto the bank, and her mended night-dress shone clean and white. It too was dry in a second and she pulled it on quickly, cherishing the warm cotton as it covered her modesty. When she sat down to rest she also noticed that the scratches on her ankles and feet were completely gone, healed in an instant, as was the bruising on her breasts which she refused to think of. It was as though her entire body had been cleansed, inside and out, and as she sat and watched the silver ripples she wished that she could stay inside this dream forever, that she would never wake up and could live peacefully in the forest for all eternity, befriending the animals like the heroes of so many of her childhood books.

Bethany slept then, right there beside the stream. She slept for a long, long time and as she slept the Blackhart felt her anguish and granted her wish, pleased to gain a companion with such an innocent soul and such a powerful mind. For though the waters of its heart were full of a deep and magical glamour, the healing force had come from the girl herself, and the forest was intrigued by this small human. She had run straight into it's centre without stirring the boar who viciously guarded the path, and she had washed in it's own lifeblood without causing any pain or wrath to surface. She was obviously very special, and the Blackhart decided there and then that it would never again allow any harm to befall this special girl, that from now on she was protected and would know only peace and beauty and the harmony of life.

When Bethany regained consciousness she had somehow moved to a small cave, where she lay on a soft bed of bracken and hay. A shivering fox-cub crouched awkwardly in the corner, back legs twisted and covered in blood, and her heart filled instantly with compassion and tenderness. She remembered nothing from her previous life, and did not even think it strange that the seasons had changed, that it was summer now and the sun was hot and high in the vast blue sky. She carried the poor cub down to the stream and twenty minutes later he could run again, and though she smiled at his happy frolicking she felt tired and her head was aching, so she wandered across to the huge oak tree and rested in the shade of it's boughs, leaning back against the cool bark of it's massive trunk. It was then that she heard a peculiar rushing noise, low and fuzzy but clearly discernible like a deep and wondrous voice inside her mind, and as the days went by she learnt the language of the forest, of the movement of the sap inside the tree, and she learnt to love the giant oak, which was the first of all the trees in the Blackhart, the Father of them all, and she named it Elan.

She learnt too that the creatures of the forest would come to her for healing and for comfort, and she cared for them all, but the little fox cub which she had saved on that very first day became more than just a creature to her, returning often to sleep by her side or just to play for a while, and so she named him Chaver.

Katrina, deep inside her sister's mind, felt all these things, and she smiled at the two names which had been chosen, remembering the lessons in Hebrew they have both been forced to endure as small children. Bethany had always said they were boring and silly, with words too weird to pronounce and meanings too old-fashioned to understand. But she had obviously retained some memories of her past, however well hidden, for she had unknowingly named her two friends in Hebrew and Katrina thought how proud their parents would have been to see her grow up to use the old language, despite all the bizarre circumstances.

Aside from the names she had chosen, Bethany's immersion in her new life was intense and overwhelming. Katrina felt the tranquillity which infused her sister's simple existence, but she also felt a nagging insistence that not everything was as perfect as it seemed. Bethany drank from the silver stream but she barely ate, as though food were unnecessary now, as though she was not quite real anymore, as though she had become another entity. Her thoughts were only of the forest, of the trees and the flowers, of the birds and the butterflies and the animals she watched over. Occasionally, there was an attempt to recapture what came before, but the images were muddled and warped inside her mind, and she found it impossible to concentrate with such a strong life-force all around her, with so many wonderful distractions of nature to keep her occupied. Time was irrelevant in the Blackhart, and she hardly noticed the years pass by, but then one day everything changed. She felt the heart-beat of an enemy, and suddenly she was scared and confused and the only thing she knew was a name: Richard Dean Haley, and it terrified her.

Katrina saw it all. She watched in sorrow and pity as the scarrings were planned, she saw the incredible truth of how they were achieved and she saw the immense hatred borne by the Blackhart towards the man she had loved so dearly. It was easy now to see how she had been so wrong, how the evil she had perceived inside the forest was not *of* the forest, but was an evil created by man, by *her* man, and she choked on the bitterness of it all.

Bethany too was saddened and dismayed to see her life laid out so cruelly before her. She held on until the moment came when she had found the girl called Gemma and been unable to raise her, but the pain of that memory overwhelmed her and, with a sharp cry, she snapped the cord which held them to the past. Katrina saw the agony in her sister's eyes at once and understood how deeply she had felt the death of her last victim, how sorry she had been, and still was, how little she truly comprehended what she had actually done to the girls she was trying to help. She pulled Bethany close and let her cry against her shoulder, wondering what to do, what to say. And as she wondered her eyes met Richard's and she wished they hadn't, for her love had turned to hate with an ease that frightened even her and she felt him recoil at the glance as though the venom he saw in her look had actually spat in his face. She turned away instantly and thought only of Bethany, of the dangerous innocence which sat weeping at her side, and so she never noticed the tears upon *his* face, she never noticed that his soul had been torn in two at the sight of his younger self committing such a terrible act, she never noticed that he slunk away quietly, unable to cope with the stark display of hatred he had glimpsed in the eyes of the woman he adored. Richard Dean Haley walked off alone into the depths of the forest, and though Katrina didn't notice, though Bethany didn't notice, the Blackhart noticed everything, and the sap of the Father Tree, the mammoth life-force of the one she had named Elan, sent out signals of fury to it's sons and to it's daughters, until the leaves of every tree and bush seethed with the passion of revenge, until all the creatures of the earth and of the sky were alert with the throes of the hunt.

Twilight had fallen in the forest, it was 'fairyland time', and as Richard heard the lilt of his sister's childhood voice in his head he also felt the change all around him, and he knew there would be no fairies tonight, for he was lost in the forest yet again, and no matter how logical he tried to be there was only one thing he knew for certain: the forest was alive, and it wanted him dead.

23

The search

At the mention of Haley's name, Hobbs looked up from his chicken sandwich and raised an enquiring eyebrow at his boss. He saw Cummings' expression change sharply and waited patiently for an explanation when the Sergeant put the phone down. He didn't get one. Instead, Cummings picked the phone back up and, after a moment of obvious scrolling to find the right name, put it to his ear again. Clearly, whoever he was trying to call was not answering and, as he put the handset back on his desk pensively, Hobbs finally voiced his curiosity.

"Well?"

Cummings looked up, seeming to notice the Constable for the first time, "Well what?"

"Jesus, Serge, do I have to drag it out of you? Who was that? What's going on with Haley?"

"Oh, right, yes. Haley." Cummings got to his feet and continued to look worried. "Yes. Very foolish young man isn't he? Yes, foolish. Indeed." He put on his jacket and threw his car keys over to Hobbs. "You want to drive then? Yes. Good. Lets be off then, quick smart." DC Hobbs just stared at him, puzzled irritation showing clearly on his broad young face.

"Well don't just stand there Hobbs! Are you waiting for something? No. Well let's go then." And he marched briskly from the room, leaving the Constable trailing behind muttering obscenities under his breath.

In the car, Cummings finally explained the call from Katrina and Hobbs was instantly agitated at the idea of Haley even setting foot in the forest again, after all that had happened, and especially after he had been strongly advised not to go anywhere near the place. He immediately requested back up for a full manhunt but Cummings was adamant this was unnecessary, proclaiming that he was more concerned for Haley's safety than for anything else. Hobbs was immensely annoyed at the Sergeant's refusal to suspect his new-found friend in the Scarrings case but when he made his feelings known Cummings just annoyed him even more with a condescending laugh and an emphatic shake of the head.

"Oh for God's sake Serge, you don't have to be so patronising. Just because you like the guy doesn't mean he's not the one. You know as well as I do that lots of murderers and rapists and... whatever this guy is.....can seem very nice when you talk to them, but these sort of people are expert con-men. And besides, half of them are so messed up they don't even realise what they've actually done most of the time." He sighed sulkily as he stared out at the road ahead. "I just don't understand why you don't get it. You must be the only person in this whole damn town who doesn't see him for the maniac that he really is."

Cummings smiled again and looked bemused at the Constable's outburst. He didn't 'get it' because, as far as he was concerned, there was nothing *to* get. He felt he knew Richard Haley very well by now, and his first impressions - that he was just a soft-hearted teacher with a penchant for running through trees - had been amply verified. The only thing that worried him about the man was his ridiculous obsession with the so-called 'barefooted girl', who may or may not be a real person, and the fact that, as Hobbs had just pointed out, the whole town believed him to be a monster. And on a day like today, with emotions flying high from the funeral, the main thing that frightened him was the idea that someone might have seen him going into the Blackhart. He had always had his doubts about Haley's bizarre stories of his forest mishaps, and had often wondered if he hadn't just experienced a good old-fashioned beating at the hands of vigilantes. That scenario made a lot more sense to him than stumbling across the lair of a wild boar or an army of angry foxes. But again, on a day like today, a beating would not be enough, he felt, and he almost expected to find an angry mob already tearing up the forest path when they reached the Blackhart's entrance.

"Shall we just be realistic for a moment, Hobbs? Yes. Right then. What actual evidence do you have that Mr Haley is anything more than the soppy schoolteacher that he is, according to you, only *posing* as?" He let the silence speak for itself before answering his own question, as usual. "None. Exactly. None whatsoever. Absolutely nothing. Diddely-squat, as they say. Just like the rest of this dreadful case. And until we do have a single tiny shred of real hard evidence, I am sticking to my guns and resting assured that the Blackhart Scarrer is not, and never has been, Mr Richard Haley." He paused and took a deep breath. "Anything further you wish to add, Hobbs? No. Good. Then kindly shut up."

The rest of the drive was conducted in complete silence as the Constable took his aggression out on the car, driving fast enough to give himself a speeding ticket and sounding the horn loudly at the smallest inconvenience. When they arrived at the entrance to the forest Hobbs slammed the door open, stamped outside and slammed it shut again. Cummings simply sighed and resigned himself to the company of an irate underling for the rest of the day. He was, by now, quite used to the young DC's exasperation and had learnt to ignore it, just as he had learnt to ignore similar comments from the rest of his officers. He seemed to be the only person in the force who did not believe in the guilt of Mr. Haley, and whilst his superiors were well aware that they had no grounds on which to arrest him, their feelings were made clear at every opportunity, and the Sergeant was shunned for having made a friend of everyone else's enemy.

However, as they strode down the pathway and into the Blackhart, Hobbs' anger began to diminish. In the car he had been wishing he could go in on his own, had been desperate for the chance to rent his fury on Haley once he was found, but as they stepped on the soft earth for the first time he knew he was glad of the Sergeant's company. The forest was quiet and calm but there was a crackle in the air, a vague vibration of unease which convinced him that all was not as peaceful as it seemed. They both felt it immediately, though neither made a comment, and as they walked they glanced at each other too often, checking for the security of someone else beside them, each grateful he was not alone. The two PC's who were supposed to be on patrol along the main path were nowhere to be seen and Cummings made a mental note to reprimand them later. He guessed at their boredom, at their perpetual discomfort at being in the place that everyone feared, and he understood why they were not here. But he also knew that he would brook no excuses. Though their job was tedious and somewhat intimidating, it was also extremely important, and if anything happened here today which they could have prevented he would make them wish they had never been born.

Hobbs, on the other hand, had not even noticed the lack of a police presence. He was far too busy concentrating on remembering which paths they were taking, marking tree positions in his head, taking stock of any unusual flowers or strangely shaped shrubs which would remind him later of the direction they had chosen. He prided himself on an excellent homing instinct, on the fact that he had never yet got lost in this monotonous landscape, unlike many of his colleagues over the past few weeks, but he wasn't averse to helping that instinct a little, so he stayed alert and built a map in his mind so that if needs be he could retrace his steps as easily as if he had left a trail of bread crumbs behind him. When the darkness came, so sudden and unexpected, he stopped moving, his attention distracted by the bizarre change, and he looked directly at Cummings as if expecting an explanation.

"What's going on?"

"How should I know, Hobbs. It just went dark. That's all."

"But that's ridiculous. I mean, it's still early. Why would it be dark?"

"For God's sake Hobbs, it probably just clouded over or something. Pull yourself together young man. You're not afraid of the dark are you? No. Of course not. Now lets move it along shall we?"

Hobbs stared at his Sergeant in outright disbelief, amazed at the older man's abject refusal to admit that something incredibly weird had just happened.

"I'm sorry Sir but," he paused, clearly contemplating the sanity of uttering the word which came most naturally to his tongue, "well... Bullshit, actually Sir. That's total bullshit and you know it. It's dark as in night-time dark, not just a bit grey 'cause there's a few clouds up there. There's a big difference between the two and we both know that this is bloody peculiar so why don't you just stop hiding behind your stupid attempts at rationalising everything and actually dare to entertain the idea that this place is *fucking creepy as hell*!"

Hobbs took a deep breath as his outburst ended and looked miserably down at his feet, knowing only too well that he had gone too far this time, that no matter what he may think of his boss, Sergeant Cummings was an excellent Detective and should be treated with the respect he deserved. He waited for a strong rebuttal but when none was instantly forthcoming he decided that a swift apology could do no harm at this point.

"I'm sorry Sir, I was out of order there. Please accept my apologies. This place is just getting to me, I guess."

He continued to look down at his feet and Cummings surprised him by patting his back casually before moving on. He spoke as they walked and clicked on a large torch which lit up the scenery with an eerie yellow glow.

"Don't you worry young man, it's a strange old place the Blackhart, you think I don't know that? Yes? Well you're wrong. Always been a strange one this, but that doesn't mean we have to go around believing in all kinds of nonsense, does it? No, it doesn't. There's always a logical reason for things Hobbs, you mark my words. Yes, always a reason, even if you can't work it out right away. So, in this case, maybe there's a storm brewing and these big trees are blocking out what little light there is left out there. Forests are a law unto their own you know, have their own weather and their own weird and wonderful ways. It's called nature, young man, and it doesn't fit into nice neat little boxes like all those tidy file-box thingamys you have on your desk."

He smiled at the Constable and Hobbs smiled back, recognising the subtle dig at his obsessive neatness which everyone at the station found highly amusing. His outburst was forgotten and they wandered together through the woodland with a newly relaxed atmosphere, searching every area with sickly amber torch-light as they walked. It was a long-winded, time-consuming job but the deeper they strode into the forest the more convinced Cummings became that Haley was in danger again, that they needed to find him soon, before anyone else did.

They chatted as they walked, small-talk mostly, never about the Scarrings, never about Haley, and as the hours passed they could skirt the issue no longer. They had found nothing and no-one. Surely it was time to go back.

They both agreed to give up the search and Cummings was glad to let Hobbs lead the way out of the labyrinth of trees which he had come to loathe. He was very grateful for the young Constable's impeccable memory, and said so, as he knew he would be utterly lost by now without his help. But it seemed he had spoken too soon, and when Hobbs announced he had taken a wrong turn the Sergeant began to feel truly afraid for the first time in his life. The yellow glare of the torch had become quite sinister and when they tried to double back they discovered they had merely circled the same area and were right back to where they had started from. The darkness had become uncannily oppressive as the hour had grown late and the two men searched in ominous silence for a way through the tangle of thorny shrubs at their feet and the looming branches overhead. When they came across the corpse it was a shock to them both and as Hobbs stumbled backwards he caught his foot against the Sergeant's ankle and they both went down.

"Oh God, not again." Hobbs covered his face with his hands and stayed on the ground, not wanting a second look, dreading another victim with Hell for a face, another death for a town still in mourning for the first. Cummings sprang straight back on his feet though, not so easily affected by the sight of mortality, and shone the light directly at her face as he checked for a pulse professionally, despite being sure that there was none.

"It would appear not, Constable. I think this is something altogether different." He frowned deeply, bending closer to see the tiny puncture wounds on the dead girls cheeks and the scratches on her thighs and the tops of her arms. As he leaned in, the phone in his pocket sung out the Bond theme and, startled, he jumped upright at once, muttering about heart attacks as he fumbled for the handset before answering with a harsh "What?"

"It's all over Sergeant. I just wanted to let you know."

"Miss Rose? What's all over? Where are you? Where's Haley?"

"Everything. Everything's over. The scarrings .. Richard .. everything." She broke off, a sob in her throat and he heard her catch it before she continued. "I'm at home. I have no idea where Richard is and I don't honestly care. But I could use some company if you want the truth. And I can tell you all about it. The whole thing. Not that you'll believe a word but, hey, you've nothing better to believe have you. Maybe it's time somebody broadened that narrow mind of yours."

She tried to laugh but started crying instead and Cummings was momentarily lost for words. He looked down at the body by his feet and across at Hobbs, who had managed to stand and was staring at the dead girl with clear confusion. It suddenly struck him that she was dressed only in a thin cotton night-dress and had nothing on her feet, and he realised that the body they had stumbled across was none other than Haley's 'barefooted girl', which gave him cause to doubt his own judgement of the teacher's good character, especially if his previously devoted girlfriend was now

216

completely unconcerned for his well-being.

"Miss Rose I .. Well, I don't quite know if I should be telling you this but it seems that the present circumstances dictate it so there we are. We, that is Detective Constable Hobbs and myself, are currently in the Blackhart and have found..." He trailed off, aware of protocol but also aware of Miss Rose's conviction that Haley's mysterious girl in the forest was her sister, and feeling somehow that she had a right to know that the girl in question was no longer alive, despite the fact that this body belonged to a teenager and could not possibly be Bethany Rose no matter how much she looked like her. But that was the problem, she did look like her, she looked *exactly* like her in every single way. Cummings had known Bethany Rose, had met her, spoken to her, had helped to scour the forest for her all those years before with a small photograph of her in his breast pocket just in case it was at all conceivable that he could forget the lovely, guileless smile she always wore and those deep, soulful eyes which always reminded him of babies. And though her eyes were closed now, the slight uplift in her lips bore a faint suggestion of that smile he had searched so hard to find, and his rational mind turned cartwheels in his head as he tried in vain to find a logical answer to what his eyes were trying to tell him.

"We've found the body of a young girl, I'm afraid," he suddenly blurted out, shrugging at Hobbs as he spoke and receiving a similar shrug in return, "and, well, it .. *she* .. matches the description given by Mr Haley of the girl he encountered whilst ..."

"Yes I know that Sergeant," Katrina cut him off quickly but gently, "and I would beseech you to leave her be, if you have an ounce of compassion in you. The forest takes care of it's own, Mr Cummings, and I beg you to respect that, to respect her last wishes, and to respect the wishes of her next of kin. And if you can't do that then you won't be welcome here at all, Sergeant, and the Blackhart Scarrer will remain a mystery to you forever. So please, for her sake, for mine and for your own, please leave her be. OK?"

Cummings shook his head and the frown deepened. He was lost and there was a dead body lying prone and semi-naked on the ground below him. Hobbs had finally turned away and was visibly shivering, either from the chill of the night air or from their recent discovery, and the woman on the other end of the phone had just told him that the most difficult, most heat-rending case of his entire career was finished, that she had the answer to it all, but that to hear it he must disregard his training and his job and leave this poor dead girl exposed in the dark, cold and alone, a waiting meal for the scavengers of the night. What had she said, 'the forest takes care of it's own'?.

"I really don't know if I can do that. Miss Rose. To leave her here? No. It's just not right, is it? No. But last wishes you say? Next of kin? This is all very....." He stopped, confused but somehow relenting, "OK. But I don't know what time I'll get there. We're completely lost at the moment and I'll have to sort a few things out with young Hobbs here. By God, Miss Rose, do you realise what you're asking of me? Yes, I thought so. But I wish you could explain things right now I really do." He sighed and glanced over at Hobbs who was beginning to show his impatience. "Actually, young lady, why can't you explain things now? I really do feel that would be best. At least give me a name, yes?"

"No, Sergeant, I'm sorry. It's going to be difficult enough to convince you as it is. But if I start trying to explain on the phone you'll probably just hang up on me. So, do you want to get out of the Blackhart or what? Yes. Good." She copied his own tactics to prevent an argument and left no pause for interruptions. "Then turn to your left and walk about ten steps forward then turn right and keep going straight. That should bring you out on the school short-cut and you'll know where you are. I'll see you shortly."

The connection was broken and he put the phone back in his pocket. Hobbs was waiting for direction, was desperate to have an order to follow or anything at all to do to keep him from thinking. He could not help wondering why it was always him that found the dead girls, and he wished he had eaten his lunch somewhere else for a change, instead of at his desk like the foolish workaholic he had become. So when Cummings took the lead, with a brash and unconvincing show of confidence, the relief showed on his face and he followed the Sergeant without a word until they reached the pathway. By then, of course, his curiosity had got the better of him and he wanted to know everything. Why hadn't they called in to report the body? What had Haley's girlfriend told him? How had he known which way to go when they had been so lost? So many questions, so much confusion, and Cummings decided that the only way to keep the Constable quiet was to let him tag along with him to see Katrina Rose, who apparently was going to make everything crystal clear so that they could all finally get to sleep at night. Hobbs seemed happy with that solution but hated the idea that Haley was still out there somewhere. The drive to Richard's house was short and fast, with the Constable at the wheel once more, but when they got there the house was as dark as the forest they had left behind, and their repeated knocking attracted no-one but the man next door, who peered nosily through his bedroom curtains and hurriedly woke his wife to spread the gossip. Initially, Cummings was at a loss, but then he realised that when his phone had rung in the

Blackhart it had simply displayed a number, rather than 'Haley', and he recognised their mistake in a flash.

"Of course," he said, "she's at *home*, not here," and he snatched the car keys from Hobbs' hand, "I'll drive."

24

Sisters

When Bethany stopped crying she pulled away from her sister and looked around her, eyes wide and flickering from one shadow to another in the darkening night. Chaver instantly ran to her side, pushing his head onto her hand tenderly, and she stroked his rough fur with obvious affection.

"It's starting," she announced suddenly "I can feel it already." And she tried to stand but Katrina caught her quickly as her legs gave way beneath her.

"It's OK Bethie, sit down," she answered, anxious to finally look after her little sister as she should, "What's starting?"

"Don't call me Bethie. My name is Bethany. Will you help me now? I need to go somewhere. Please?"

Katrina nodded, "Of course," but she didn't understand, "we can go home now, that's right, you don't have to stay here anymore." She helped Bethany to her feet and the young girl looked up at her, a strange mixture of sorrow and eagerness in her expression.

"No, my sister, this is my home, the forest. I can never leave. I have no desire to leave. But I am growing weaker every moment and there is a place I must go to rest. Can you help me walk there? It is not far."

Katrina looked hurt and confused but she knew she could not refuse her sister's wish and they began to walk, Bethany pointing the way while her feet dragged along the ground and her breathing became more shallow with every movement. The air was cooler now, the moon the only light, and as Katrina all but carried her sister she felt the young girl's skin turn cold and pale, and saw the spark in her eyes grow dimmer as she wheezed. She still had no idea why they couldn't just go home but she realised she had no right to place demands upon someone she had wronged so much in the past, so she stayed quiet and hoped beyond hope that everything was going to be all right.

When Bethany motioned for her to stop it took a minute for Katrina to recognise where she had brought them. Then she nearly screamed, and as her sister slid to the ground she knelt beside her, dismayed and bewildered.

"My God Bethany. Why on earth would you want to come here? I mean, Jesus sweetheart, why?"

Bethany found it hard to speak aloud but she could still think clearly, so when she answered inside Katrina's head it was with images as well as words, in an attempt to ease her sister's worried mind as much as she could.

"Do not be afraid, my sister, for this is not only a place of pain, it is a place of change. Do you not see how I was remade here? How a new soul was born amidst the blood and the screams. When new life is created there is always pain, it is the way of all things." She lay down as if to sleep and still Katrina did not understand. The questions and the fear in her mind were easy to read and Bethany acknowledged that her sister did not want to understand, that she was trying hard to fight the truth and to refuse reality, though she knew it could not be beaten.

"What are you talking about sweetheart?" She smiled down at the tired, angelic face resting below her, "I'm here now. I came to save you. We can go home and start another new life, together. Can't we? Please say we can? Or if you want to stay here then... then that's fine but I need to know that I can come and see

222

you every day. I can bring you clothes and food and we can talk and..." She blinked back tears and stifled a sob. "Please say it's going to be OK?"

Bethany found the strength to smile back at her and filled her mind with images of peace and of beauty. "It's over now, my sister, and I am so tired. I have been tired for so long now, so tired, so lonely and so uncertain. But now, at last, I can be free. Free from all the tangles in my mind and all the aches in my heart. Do you not see? Everything *is* OK. This is what should be, this is what I want, what I *need*." The flow of thoughts stopped for a moment and Katrina could hold her tears no longer. She was living her nightmare for real this time and it was hurting so much more than she had expected. 'Don't go!' Her head screamed. 'Please don't go, I need to feel you. What will I do if I can't feel you anymore? How will I live? I can't live!'

But her sister squeezed her hand and showed her the forest. She showed her the trees and the leaves they bore and the blossom that bloomed in the spring time. She showed her the twigs that crackle underfoot and the soft earth which nourishes the bluebells and the sweet violet and the foxgloves where the sun shines the brightest.

"There is a poem, I think, which says you will find me in all these things. I have some memory of a poem, but it is all fading now. I am fading, my sister, but I will always be here. You should go now, it is almost time, and you must not let them move me. The forest takes care of it's own, Katrina, dear sister, and it will take care of me, but if you want to save Richard you must go quickly."

Katrina shuddered as she heard his name and wondered with fresh amazement at the extent of her sister's compassion.

"I don't care about him, I care about you. I don't

even want to think of him again so why should I want to save him?"

With immense effort, Bethany managed to open her eyes and she stared straight into those of her sister as if to bore into her very soul.

"He did not know, Katrina. Did you not see?" And she filled her thoughts with the madness and rage of the Blackhart, until Katrina cried out from the terror which had poured unbidden into her brain. "He will die without you, and it will be soon. The forest will take us both if you do not go now." And she tried to push her sister away with what little power remained in her. Katrina choked on her grief and kissed Bethany's forehead gently. The concept of leaving her there alone was one she dared not dwell on, but she knew she would have to do exactly that, for she could not let her sister think that she was going to disregard her dying wish.

"I love you Bethany, I always have." She whispered as she stood and then she watched with a flood of relief as the raggedy old fox she now recognised as Chaver sprung forward, seemingly out of nowhere. He settled down beside Bethany and as he did so she sent forth a new image into her sister's mind. A bright and beautiful picture of the Blackhart and all who dwelt within its magical boundaries. And in the centre of the image was a young barefooted girl, carefree and smiling, cradling a fox-cub in her arms and waving happily as she turned away and strolled through the trees. Katrina smiled as she wept, and Bethany watched her leave before her eyes closed for the last time.

Later, barely conscious, she murmured too softly. That was all.

25

Frankie

Richard was finished. He had walked and run and tripped and run and stumbled and crawled and wept and screamed and crawled some more until he could no longer move for the pain in his limbs and his heart. The forest was finally going to win and he could not fight anymore, did not want to fight anymore, for he knew he could not live with the knowledge of what he had done all those years ago. The tree roots bound his legs and the birds snatched at his hair while the insects stung and the creatures attacked with a ferocity he would not have believed just a few short weeks ago when everything was normal. He squealed in agony as the teeth ripped his skin and the squirming mass of fur across his body tore into him with excruciating force. It would not be long now, he knew, for there was too much blood and too much pain and please God let it be over soon, please God I'm so sorry, I'm so sorry.....

But suddenly it was over. Only he was still alive. The blood dripped from countless wounds and one eye dangled against his cheek and he sobbed and wheezed and prayed to God to let him die. The creatures had all gone, the trees were just trees again and he was alone. This was his penance, he thought, to die slowly and in so much pain, and he deserved every second but God it was so bad, he never knew anything could hurt so much. He felt a brush of fur against his hand and his heart rose in expectation as he hoped they were back to finish him off. But the fur rubbed again, harder this time and he heard a purring sound that took his breath away.

"Frankie? Frankie is that you?" his words were barely audible but the kitten began to mew and purr and rub even harder until Richard realised that the pain was subsiding and the blood no longer flowed. Somehow, Frankie was making him well again and his tortured soul relaxed until his brain relented and switched off completely. He would wake one day, anew, and by then the forest would know what to do. For the moment, though, a new innocent soul had appeared, a small black cat with love in his heart who had cried out to save their enemy and made it impossible for them to destroy him. Despite its diminutive size the little cat was strong and pure of spirit and the forest watched as it worked to heal this hated man-creature. If such a virtuous soul could love this foe then maybe he should not be foe anymore, maybe he could be of use with his speed and his strength, and the cat could be a new healing presence now that the girl had been reclaimed by the earth. So the forest watched and waited, as it had always done, and the man who had been Richard Dean Haley slept and healed with a small black cat by his side.

26

Reality

The Rose house was nothing like he remembered it. He almost didn't knock, so doubtful was he of his memory when faced with such disparity. The front garden, always immaculate with expertly pruned roses, was a wilderness of weeds and overgrown bushes, and if he hadn't seen the crack of light through the curtains he may well have turned away. The inside of the house had also undergone great change. Gone were the polished surfaces and delicate ornaments, in their place an array of dust and candles amongst the mess of magazines and paperbacks. Against such a turbulent background Katrina looked even more beautiful than usual, and Cummings wondered briefly if the mess was deliberate, before realising that of course it was, but not for that reason. Here was a woman at ease with her looks yet completely devoid of vanity and the chaos was chosen because, for her, neatness and boredom had become synonymous.

At the start, when she had cleared a space on the cluttered sofa for them both to sit down, Katrina curled her legs into a big leather chair and smoked in silence, sipping brandy and staring at nothing. It was as though she was trying to decide what they were doing in her house, why she had invited them at all and how she could make them leave as quickly as possible. Hobbs, ever impatient, was the first to demand an explanation, and she looked at him as if he were a stranger, making a point to finish her cigarette before she began. When she finally spoke she directed her attention mainly towards Sergeant Cummings, only glancing at the

Constable now and then as if to reinforce his attention. After a while, however, it became obvious that Cummings was a lost cause. His expression declared his disbelief as fully as if he were shouting "BOLLOCKS" through a megaphone, and she picked up on this instantly, shifting her focus entirely to Hobbs, who sat transfixed and amazed, wondering why he felt so keenly that this impossible nonsense was nonetheless true. He too saw that Cummings was not impressed, and he knew he should feel the same way. In fact, he realised that a month ago he would have felt exactly the same way. But he had never forgotten that night in the forest when something had spooked him, and he would never forget the endless hours of searching and the peculiar 'accidents' which many of his colleagues and friends had suffered. And, most of all, he would never forget the face of Gemma Cooke, the bloodless hue of her delicate skin; and he would never forget the fragile perfection of the face they had just left behind in the Blackhart, the very same face which stared at him now from the ornate silver frame on the mantelpiece. No matter how hard he tried, he could not convince himself that the two girls were different people, and if they were not, then the story he was hearing may as well be genuine, for that was just as impossible as anything else he had heard tonight, and he knew he believed it.

When she had finished he had the grace to look away as she dried her eyes and sniffed into a tissue. It was a sad story, and he did not blame her for crying. In fact, what he most wanted to do was to put his arms around her and hold her close, to tell her that he understood, that her sister was at peace now and that everything was going to be just fine. But of course he could not do that. Who was he to comfort her after all she'd been through? A useless cop who had done

228

nothing to help, who had only lost his temper and ransacked her boyfriend's house for no good reason. Cummings also had enough respect to wait until she had composed herself, but then he ruined everything by asserting his scepticism forcefully.

"You seem to think, Miss Rose, that I should believe all this poppycock, is that right? Yes. Well I can only assume that you have taken leave of your senses young lady." He shook his head and gave her a disparaging glare. "Good Grief. I haven't heard such rot since my mother used to tell me bedtime stories. Now, if you and Mr Haley have had some sort of row or he's confessed to a crime of some kind, then that's one thing. But to invent all this rubbish about your poor sister? Well, I can't condone that. No, I certainly can't." He continued to shake his head and clearly avoided looking up at the picture of Bethany Rose which sat right in front of them. Katrina noticed this and was not in the least disturbed by his refusal to accept the truth. She uncurled her legs and reached over to pick up the photograph.

"This is Bethany, Sergeant. I mean, I do know my own sister, and if I remember rightly you knew her fairly well yourself." She threw the picture straight at him so he had no choice but to catch it, and as he looked down uncomfortably at the smiling young girl it portrayed she saw clear recognition in his eyes and his frown deepened considerably.

"Well, yes, I admit the resemblance is uncanny but logic dictates that that is all it can be. You must see that? Yes? Just a striking resemblance." He stood up and placed the picture back in the exact same position it had come from. His feet seemed to shuffle nervously as he moved, quite out of character, and she sensed he was building up to the one question she did not want to answer. Quickly, she turned to Hobbs before anyone could speak.

"You've been very quiet, D C Hobbs. Which from what I recall isn't like you at all." Her eyes flashed playfully as Cummings returned to his seat and continued to fidget anxiously. "So what do you think? Am I making all this up for some bizarre reason? Or maybe I have, what was it Sergeant?, 'taken leave of my senses', and you should cart me straight off to the nut-house. Is that what you think?"

Hobbs looked up at the dazzling beauty before him and for a moment he could not speak, so struck was he by her bewitching appearance. He wondered why he had not noticed her like this before and he realised that he had never actually looked at her properly until this moment, that previously he had always concentrated on Mr Haley, on spotting the chink in his armour of deceit which would lead to his arrest. But now all his theories had been smashed up and thrown away, and he was left with this tantalising vision who knew all the answers. She stared at him expectantly and he swallowed hard.

"Well?"

He cleared his throat and glanced at Cummings before looking back at her. He didn't want to believe any of it, but he knew she wasn't lying and he knew she was as sane as he was. So he took a deep breath and prepared to annoy his boss yet again.

"Well, I.. I'm not usually one for believing in ghosts or whatever, and I did have my heart set on making an arrest for all this dreadful business, but I have to say that I don't think you're any more mad than I am, Miss Rose, and if everything you just said was a lie then you should be in Hollywood." He almost smiled but caught the Sergeant's cold expression and cleared his throat again instead. He watched Cummings roll his eyes before turning back to her. "And besides, apart from any of that, the first thing I saw when I walked in here was a photograph of the lovely young lass we just found in the forest just now? And while I might want to try and rationalise all this, I can't deny what I've seen with my own eyes. And it's your sister I've just seen, Miss Rose, I wish it wasn't but it is. And quite frankly I find it much more ridiculous that there's another girl out there who just happens to look exactly like her."

"Have you quite finished?" Cummings was quietly fuming and could no longer keep his exasperation in check. "I took you for an intelligent man, Hobbs. I have no idea how you can sit there and spout such rubbish. My God man, just listen to yourself for a minute! Magical healing powers? Trees that move on command? Bird ghosts and other such twaddle?" He stared at Hobbs, truly astounded, more outraged that his Constable could believe Katrina's story than at the story itself. But Hobbs simply shrugged and returned the stare, clearly amazed himself at his own acceptance of such a bizarre account.

"What's that saying?" They both looked at the young man as he spoke, puzzled and expectant. "You know, there's a saying, a quote from something I think. Goes like: 'There are more things in heaven and earth...' Damn, I can't remember the rest, never was much good with words but..."

"Hamlet, Act One, Scene Five 'There are more things in heaven and earth, Horatio, than are dreamt of in your philosophy' though most people don't bother with the Horatio bit." Katrina smiled at him gladly and this time he smiled back, oblivious to Cummings rolling his eyes yet again.

"That's the one. Except maybe we should replace Horatio with DS Cummings in this case." They laughed together while the Sergeant shook his head and grew increasingly irritated. He was clearly not amused and the quote was utterly lost on his cynical mind. He also found the recent frivolity entirely misplaced and quite offensive, given the seriousness of the case they were investigating. He had already decided that they had wasted enough time here and when he excused himself to make a phone call Katrina guessed what he was doing.

"They'll never find her." She spoke with confidence and with sadness and for the first time in his career Hobbs wished he wasn't a policeman. He tried to smile at her, to think of something reassuring to say, but he couldn't, and he hoped Cummings would not tell her that they had marked the route through the Blackhart as they left, that she could actually be found all too easily. To break the awkward silence as they waited for the Sergeant's return he asked her the one question she had been avoiding all night.

"So what happened to Mr Haley? You didn't really explain that part."

Katrina closed her eyes and tried not to think of Richard at all. His charming half-smile still swam in her head, but now it just looked like a leer and she felt like screaming as she clenched her fists and refused to answer. She blinked back tears as she opened her eyes and suddenly Cummings was back in the room and Hobbs rose to his feet respectfully.

"I shall be going to meet the team up at the Blackhart, Hobbs. You don't have to come with me. In fact, at the moment I'd rather you didn't if it's all the same to you? Yes. Well, I'll keep you informed, of course." He turned to Katrina, who didn't bother to stand. "And I shall be advising quite strongly that you undergo some sort of counselling, Miss Rose. I don't usually go in for that type of thing myself, but in this case I imagine it might be jolly useful. Obviously, your sister's disappearance has left some deep scars. Yes, very deep scars I'm sorry to say. Anyway, get some sleep young lady, I'll see myself out."

They heard the front door click shut and Hobbs remained standing, clearly uncomfortable.

"There goes my transport I'm afraid. I'll have to call a cab if you'll excuse me. Would it be OK if I waited here until it arrives?"

"Yes, of course. In fact you can spend the night if you want. And don't look so terrified, I mean in one of the guest rooms." She practically twinkled with mischief and he wondered how she was coping so well. Then he realised that the ashtray was full and the glass of brandy she continually sipped from never seemed to get any emptier. He sighed and looked down at his feet, anything to avoid that enchanting face of hers. He had no idea what to say but he felt it would be terribly unprofessional not to leave, so he gestured to his mobile and turned to walk from the room.

Suddenly, she jumped up and grabbed his arm, and his stomach lurched at the feel of her hand.

"Don't go." She seemed desperate, frightened almost, and his heart melted at once. Then she must have seen the softness in his eyes for she hardened instantly and flinched away from him

"I mean, don't bother with a cab, you can take my car. I'm not exactly going anywhere tonight am I?" Then something struck her. "Shit! Oh, sorry," she glanced at him nervously, somehow feeling it was wrong to swear in front of a police officer, "it's just that I do need to go somewhere. Oh, bugger! You couldn't give me a lift could you? I mean, I'm really sorry, but it's just that I forgot all about Frankie and he'll be starving by now." She started rummaging around through the chaos which served as a living room and managed to unearth her handbag and a set of keys, though Hobbs could not imagine where they had appeared from. She seemed to be panicking out of all

233

proportion but then he had no idea who Frankie was and his startled expression of bewilderment must have amused her for she suddenly stopped and burst out laughing.

"What's up with you? I take it you don't approve of my housekeeping, or lack thereof?"

"No, no, that's not..." he stumbled, not wanting to offend. Then he saw the stern look on her face and he gave in, "well, yes actually. I mean this place really is a tip, isn't it? I don't know how you live like this to be honest, Miss Rose. But that's not really the issue at the moment is it? So let's go and sort out Frankie, whoever that may be, and you can calm down and explain things in the car, OK?"

She visibly relaxed and he helped her blow out the candles before they left. He was very glad to find out that 'Frankie' was a kitten, and when he found out whose kitten, he was even more glad that she was not going alone.

"So if you don't know where Mr Haley is, how come you're worried about the cat, Miss Rose?"

"I'm not worried," she answered defensively, "and stop with all the 'Miss Rose' crap will you? It makes me sound like some ageing spinster. My name is Katrina."

"OK, *Katrina*, but you never did answer my question back then, and you're not answering it now either. What happened to Mr Haley?"

"I don't want to talk about Richard. Not ever. I don't want to think about him or hear his name or anything. I just want to make sure Frankie's OK." And she refused to say any more.

They didn't speak much after that. Hobbs was aware of how frayed Katrina's nerves were and, for his part, he was trying hard not to allow his attraction for her to show. They were both tired and when they reached

Richard's house they were both reluctant to leave the comfort of the car, though for different reasons. Finally, they both got out together and Katrina unlocked the front door, Hobbs staying close behind her as they walked through into the hallway. The house was in total darkness and there was no excited mewling or jingling collar-bell rushing to greet them, which was what she had expected. Puzzled, she switched on all the lights and, with Hobbs' overprotective presence forever at her side, she moved swiftly through the house, calling out 'Frankie?' and 'Ratboy?' at equal intervals and making strange chirping noises with her mouth, the cat equivalent of a whistle. Back in the hallway she was forced to admit defeat and it was then that Hobbs' phone sang out the theme from the Muppets and, ever polite, he excused himself as he answered it.

The conversation was short and clearly one-sided, with the Constable's contribution consisting mainly of "No, Sir", "I don't know, Sir", and "I really have no idea". When he had finished he turned to see Katrina sitting on the stairs with her head in her hands.

"I guess I have good news for you." She took her hands away and looked up from her tearstained face. "They didn't find her. Cummings is sure they went to the right place but there was nothing there. So I guess that's it." He shrugged and tried a consoling smile. "He's pretty pissed off, as you can imagine."

"Yeah, I bet." She tried to smile too but the best either could manage was a wry grimace. "Well, I suppose that's it then. Looks like Frankie's gone too, though how he could've got out is beyond me. I'll just check the garden." She stood up and he made to follow her but she stopped him straight away.

"I'd prefer it if you'd just wait for me here, Constable, if that's OK?"

Her beseeching gaze flattened him instantly and he

nodded his consent. "Call me Chris," he called after her without even knowing he was going to speak, and he didn't know if she had heard him.

Katrina walked out of the back door and crooned softly for the kitten she knew was gone for good. She didn't really need to check the garden to know he was gone, but she had found it strange that all his food and toys were still there, just no cat. Yet she had wanted to come out here just one last time. To remind herself of it all before she wiped him from her mind completely. She had said her goodbyes to the house, to her trial of monogamy, to love; now it was time to say goodbye to the lover.

When she came back inside her eyes were dry and she seemed incredibly composed, almost too much so. He wondered how upset she was about the cat, whether it even mattered on top of everything else, but he knew he would be devastated if his cat disappeared, and he figured it was just the icing on the cake. In one night she had lost so very much, and whilst he thought he should say something to comfort her, he also thought that no words could possibly be of any comfort. So he said nothing, and he patted her arm gently, unsure of what would be appropriate.

Katrina looked at him then, grateful understanding in her eyes, and as he felt the strength in her gaze he knew that she would not let this night destroy her, he knew that she would never crumble, or fall, and he also knew that he would love her forever, this beautiful, powerful woman with fire in her hair and jewels in her eyes. And even if she could not love him back, with her next words he knew they would always be friends, and for now that was more than enough, for now that was just as it should be.

"Take me home, Chris."

27

Peace

In the darkest hour they came to her. The creatures of the night gathered for their feast and the girl would not flinch for she could no longer cry. She lay still, and calm, death in her dreams; and the black crow pecked at her face.

Epilogue

"Grandma, Grandma! Tell Sayla and Pinnie the Blackhart story. Please Grandma, tell the story, tell the story!"

"Can I hear it too, Grandma? I won't have bad dreams, honest I won't. I'm a big boy now aren't I?"

The children were excited, as usual, for they loved their Grandmother dearly and liked to hear all the stories of the old days, when cars were filled up instead of plugged in and when virtual television didn't even exist. But tonight two of Katherine's friends were staying over, and they had never heard the legend of the Blackhart Scarrer, so Katherine and Tam were eager to hear their favourite tale once again.

Their mother tutted loudly but Grandma just grinned and gathered all four children onto the sofa with her.

"Once upon a time there were four young girls who were very very pretty. They were quite different from each other but as well as being pretty, they were all very brave and independent."

"What's indee-penan?" asked Tam, who was only five.

"Oh shush Tam! It means they weren't big babies like you are." His sister pinched him for interrupting and he pinched her straight back, yelling at her loudly that he wasn't a baby and, anyway, she was just a big pig. One quick word from dad with a meaningful glance brought the skirmish to a fast end, however, and the story continued with the children suddenly on their best behaviour, eyes growing wider with fear and amazement as the tale unfolded.

When it was over mum quickly announced that she had ordered Katherine's favourite VTV show and she brought everyone else a coffee as the kids ran happily upstairs.

"Why do they always want to hear that dreadful story, Mother? And why do you insist on giving in to them every time? I know it's not easy for you, even after all this time."

She sat down beside her husband who switched off his news-vid and thanked her for the coffee. They both saw her blink back tears but she just smiled as she answered.

"It does them good to be scared of the forest, that's why. And as I've told you before, it really doesn't bother me anymore."

"Yeah right, Mother, I can see that," said her daughter sarcastically, "but if you don't have a problem talking about it then how come you never say what happened to the Scarrer himself? You always just say 'and he was never seen again', which is a total cop-out line if ever I heard one."

"Well, it might sound like a cop out but it's also the truth. I have no idea what happened to him. Or even if he actually was the Scarrer. Nothing was ever proven, you know. In fact, as far as I'm aware the case was never closed."

"But someone must know something about him, surely? People don't just disappear off the face of the earth do they?" Her son-in-law, ever the sceptic, had always been interested in the legend and took the opportunity to join in the conversation.

"Well, they don't these days, that's for sure, with all these new tracking whatnots. But in my day, yes, people could quite easily disappear." She looked pensive and slightly annoyed. "And Mr Haley? Well, like I said, no-one ever saw him again. Some say he went back to London, others say he killed himself or that he died out there in the Blackhart, lost and starving. Who knows? But what I do know is that the house he lived in was up for sale the very next day, and though it did get sold and a new couple moved in, they had to hire someone to clear out all his things. Because everything was just as he left it that night, and he never came back for anything, not even a change of clothes. In fact, the only thing missing from that house was his little black cat, and no-one ever saw that again either."

She stood up and smoothed down her skirt aggressively, clearly agitated. "Anyway, I have to use the bathroom if you'll excuse me. I'll check in on the kids before I come down, OK?"

She left the room and climbed the stairs slowly, still refusing to use the step-lift like everybody else. As she passed her granddaughter's bedroom she caught a snippet of conversation which lightened her mood and made her decide to invite a couple of her own friends round for tomorrow evening.

"So where on earth did your folks get the name Katherine from anyway? It's so old-fashioned you must really hate it."

"Oh I know. It's my Grandma's name and apparently I look a lot like she did before...well, y'know, before. Anyway, it doesn't really bother me 'cause only my mum calls me Katherine, even though I keep telling her not to, and it was Grandma that gave me the nickname Katz, which is really cool, only you have to spell it..."

"Yeah, yeah," said Tam, who had heard the next part too many times, "you spell it with a 'z', not an 's'."

The End

CPSIA information can be obtained at www.ICGtesting.com
Printed in the USA
LVOW07s0612290116

472810LV00003B/29/P